PRINT BOOKS

Jim Nash The Beginning
Gun Crazy
Gun Crazy 2
Gun Crazy 3
Fallen Angels
Last Stop to Nowhere
Revenge is Justice
Escape / Forget Me Not
Wedding Bell Blues / Breakdown
Forget Me Not
Mexico Time
LOBO
No Free Ride / Gone
Stealing America
No Escape
Blame It on Djibouti
Trouble in Paradise
Nash & Delaney Collide

Dead Reckoning
Lie Cheat Steal
Uncharted
Go-Around
Sand Storm
Harry Delaney Collection

No Way Out
Bad Girls
Bank Robber Dames

The Last President

JIM NASH

MEXICO TIME

PX DUKE

JIM NASH

MEXICO TIME

La línea

"Jim! You're bleeding," Anya said.

"Tell me something I don't know, kid."

"Why didn't you say something? We could have pulled over."

"I didn't want you to worry. In five minutes you'll be home."

"Are you going to be able to drive?" she asked.

"I guess we'll find out soon enough."

The border agent waved the van forward. Jim Nash approached in the shot-up van and forced the gearshift lever into park. He handed over the passports and waited while the agent scanned them.

"It's great to be home but I think I picked up some kind of stomach bug," he told the border guard.

The officer laughed before bending down to look into the van. "Yeah, I hear that a lot. You don't look so good if you don't mind me saying."

Anya leaned toward the window. "I think my dad got a bad shrimp taco. I told him to take it easy."

The guard's eyes shifted to the woman in the passenger seat. "Is that your daughter? Anya Quinn, is it?"

Anya looked at the border guard and smiled.

"My step-daughter. Yes. And you said her name right," Jim said. Out of the corner of my eye I saw Anya beaming an even bigger smile in the guard's direction.

"All right." He handed back the passports. "You're free to go. There's a drug store just up the road a bit if you need anything."

"Thanks. I'll check it out."

Jim put the van in gear. The transmission caught suddenly and jerked and he struggled to ease past the light.

"Wait. Stop!" the guard shouted.

ONE

Maddie Spence wasn't going to be happy. I left her—my partner in the business—in the lurch. Back in Blue Springs. She insisted on staying behind to comfort a friend after the woman was kidnapped. In fact, the whole lot of them had been kidnapped. Thanks to me and the help of a pair of good dogs, they were all free and safe.

How could Maddie refuse my request? When she said yes it didn't make me feel any better about what I was planning on doing, though. I even took Maddie's dog, Friday—with her permission, of course—and ostensibly headed off on a two-hour drive to visit old friends at their marina. It would throw her off the scent—Maddie, that is, not the dog. So after renewing my old marina friendships, I settled in at the trailer on the grounds to spend the night.

Except.

I didn't. I waited, wide awake.

When I was convinced everyone was fast asleep, I called for a ride and headed off on the first leg of my plan to reunite with my money. Over half a million dollars. In cash.

I left instructions behind to return the Packard and the dog to Maddie at Emma Mayberry's place in Blue Springs. Explained how we had been called in to solve a missing person case. That all concerned were old friends, too. And that everyone was safe and sound.

Warren and Allie and Hank and Erica, old friends who owned the marina, weren't going to be happy, either. I left them holding the bag. Or, in this case, the dog and the car. Whoever was brave enough to show up at Maddie's door with no story, no ideas, and no Jim Nash would be in for more than a grilling.

Although, I was pretty certain Maddie would be happy to see her dog again.

I had to do it that way. I couldn't put the woman I loved in danger. I knew I wouldn't be able to convince Maddie not to come with me. Knew she'd refuse all my entreaties otherwise. She was stubborn that way. Not that I wasn't. I was heading off alone, after all.

At least, that was my excuse.

Prior to being summoned to Blue Springs, I was preparing to buy the building housing our office and living quarters. I learned by accident the place was for sale. In twenty-four hours the decision was made. I signed papers for first refusal on the whole enchilada.

It was something I had to do. For Maddie. I wanted her to be comfortable in her surroundings, secure in the knowledge that if anything happened to me, she would have the finances to carry on. So yeah, I loved her and wanted the best for her. Thus the purchase of the building we worked and lived in.

A down payment was needed. It was a lot of money to keep my options open, but I was good for that. What I wasn't good for was the balance owing on the building. Oh, I had the cash, all right. A lot. There was one problem, though.

The cash was in safety deposit boxes. In Mexico. On the Mexican Baja. In Cabo San Lucas. I would have to make a trip down the Baja and back to retrieve what was rightfully mine.

I had a somewhat checkered history with Mexico. There was a marriage ceremony to a pregnant woman. It was performed by a fake padre. The woman turned out not to be my wife, eventually, when I figured it all out. An explosion on a yacht. No body. I knew that, because I searched and searched until I could look no more.

Eventually, Kara, my non-wife, showed up. Alive. With her son in tow. James. My namesake. But not my son, it turned out. Now James was safe with Erica, Kara's sister and wife to Hank, of marina fame and fortune.

So yeah, I was already in deep and getting deeper by the minute. I didn't even bring a burn phone. Maybe I'd pick one up in Mexico and give Maddie a call. You know, at least make a half-assed attempt to explain things.

Or maybe I wouldn't.

During the rush to make the buying arrangements for the office building, I made sure to get a will. And a power of attorney. All the things I'd need in case the deal in Cabo went south. Like I was planning on it going south from the beginning. Hell, I didn't even know I was heading down Mexico way before then.

Call it a bit of fortuitous planning on my part.

But was it? Even Maddie knew I wasn't capable of planning a drunken debauchery in a brewery.

So yeah. It was good fortune smiling down on me. The way I hoped it would keep smiling once I got across la frontera.

I didn't want to do it, but my hand was forced. The cartels were slowly moving into the resort towns. For too long they'd been hands-off. With their tentacles busy getting into government and law enforcement, the cartels were slow to learn how lucrative it had been for the chapulines.

Chapulines. Grasshoppers. Mexican slang for lone wolf drug dealers. Independents allowed by the cartels to work and flourish while they kept their hands off of and out of the resorts. But no more. Not since the cartels learned how much money gabacho turistas were willing to pay for cost-plus drugs on an all-inclusive vacation.

Blood soon followed. Robberies. Killings. Explosions. Beheadings. Hangings. Narcomantas. It was getting to the point where just being a tourist was an excuse to be robbed, murdered, or worse. I didn't want to dwell on the worse.

I n San Diego I arranged for a beater van. Paid for it with part of the wad of cash in my bag. Stashed the remainder in the van with the clean handgun I liberated back in Blue Springs.

The van would fit in on the Baja, where beaters were more prevalent than newer vehicles. It was dented and filthy and had a window covered in plastic. Probably someone had broken into the thing. Successfully, obviously.

The concern was for what was stashed inside the van. I had more cash than I should declare. I also had a handgun, thanks to a previous owner who convinced me it was unregistered. I had a small amount of ammunition. And two magazines. You know, for backup.

Cash and carry, here I come.

TWO

The lineup for the Otay Mesa crossing was worse than being late to exit an amusement park at closing time. Getting the green light at la línea made up for the wait. The accumulated perspiration dried up fast once I was safely across with no inspection and no questions. I got my bearings and headed south from Tijuana. It was an easy drive over a familiar road. I'd traveled it before, a long time ago.

In another life.

In Ensenada I halted on the malecón. I told myself I needed to stretch my legs, and I did. I took my time looking out over the ocean, but there was nothing there. Just as there was nothing that first time, either. No body. Nothing but splintered bits of yacht after the explosion.

That was done. Over with. It surprised me how meaningless it was now, in my present state of mind. I was happy with Maddie. Happy with our business. It was going well, too, just like our relationship.

Until now. Would she be waiting when I got back?

I made all the arrangements beforehand. A will. A power of attorney. A medical power of attorney. I figured it was the least I could do. I went to great pains to hide what I was doing. If she found out—

And one more thing. The building. I made arrangements to buy it. Had put down a small down payment. Had papers drawn up to give Maddie fifty-one percent when the deal was done.

That was why I needed to be on the Mexican Baja. I needed cash.

My old friend, César, had a place south of Ensenada. I'd be stopping there to make some arrangements prior to heading even farther south. This whole escapade was looking to take a lot longer than I originally thought, but with a bit of luck and some planning I would make it back in time to close on the deal to buy the building.

Would Maddie still be waiting?

I looked across the water one last time before climbing into the van.

THREE

I recognized César right off. He didn't recognize me. I knew by the way he walked. Casual. Cautious. One hand behind his back. Holding an automatic, most likely. These are the times Mexico was living now.

The row of pangas grounded on the beach told me César was still in the boat business. He had accumulated a few more than when I first met him. His business must be good.

I chose not to prolong it. I stepped out of the van. Kept my hands in front of me. Waist level. Palms down. César's huge smile of recognition greeted me. More grins followed by high fives and handshakes and a summons into César's beach house produced a bottle of tequila. Mamacita welcomed me with a seat at the table and a taste of food. She wasn't shy about joining in the celebration.

"It has been a long time, Jim. What brings you this way again?" César wanted to know.

I pondered how much to tell César. The man was a trusted friend, but still, this was Mexico. I hadn't been in touch for longer than I cared to remember. Alliances changed in this world of drugs, where desaparecidos and their bodies were literally piling up or hanging from bridges on a daily basis.

"I'm headed south to Cabo. Getting there isn't going to be the problem. Getting back might be," I told him, allowing him to digest that before going on. "I was wondering if I might have your help to do some custom work on the van."

César considered before answering. "You want to dress up that old beater? You must have resale in mind." He grinned, knowing something was up.

"Well, I—"

"No problemo, Jim. Of course. Whatever you need. But first you better let Mami feed you. It will take some of the buzz away from the tequila so we can get to work."

He was right about that. While he went to open up his shop, I allowed Mamacita to feed and water me. She grinned and laughed at my broken Mexican Spanish. Wanted to know if I was married yet and whether I had children.

I had to tell the truth, and she shook her head. Tisk-tisked in that way women do. Disappointed, she shooed me off to César in the workshop, but not before I helped to clear the table. She sat back and nodded with a huge grin pasted on her face. "Someone has trained you. I know it"

"You're right, Mami, someone has."

"Then you better keep her. She is good for you," Mami said.

I didn't have anything to add to that. I only nodded before heading off to César's workshop. It wasn't a huge building. Big enough to work on a vehicle without running into walls. A small lift. But everything was in order. Everything tucked away in locked cabinets. Welding supplies. Propane. Electric and hand tools.

"I see you've added quite a bit over the years."

Time flies.

"A little here. A little there. It all adds up," César admitted. "You should come down more often."

He already knew why I didn't. He waved a hand, as if to let me know he understood. He changed the subject by regarding the van already sitting over the lift. He opened doors and the hood. It allowed him to pretend to busy himself with an inspection.

"It doesn't look so bad. What is it that you need, Jim?"

"Armor."

He looked at me and whistled. "Armor." It wasn't a question.

"Armor plate, yes. Do you think you can help?"

César whistled again. "Oh si. No problemo. Help me take some measurements. When we're done I'll head into town to see what I can come up with."

That's what I liked about César. When I needed him that first time, he didn't ask a lot of questions, and he wasn't asking now.

"Both front doors for sure," I said. "And a back-plate of some kind just behind the front seats. I walked around to the front of the van. "Can we do something with this, too?"

"I don't see why not. Do you need anything else?"

I climbed into the back and took out the handgun I rescued from the trailer park in Blue Springs.

"I'll need some ammunition and two more magazines, at least. Maybe more if you can get them. And something that I can strap on that will hold them.

"That might take a little longer, my friend," he advised.

"I almost forgot. A steel plate for one back door, too. The left," I added.

"Why not do both of them? What do you think?"

"All right," I agreed. "Both back doors it is."

César walked around the van one more time. "We'll start by pulling the door panels and the upholstery.

I nodded and we went to work. It didn't take long. César had all the right tools. We each took a side and worked our way to the back. We finished by stripping the interior of the back seats. I handed over a wad of cash. He didn't bother counting before it disappeared into a pocket.

"One more thing, César."

He looked at me warily. Maybe I was stretching it. It never hurt to ask. "I'm going to need a panga."

A panga was another name for a machete. The boats were called pangas after a type of bait fish, a mullet-like fish with a knife-shaped body. The body resembled a machete. Panga, the nickname, stuck around.

"That's not a problem. You can use one of mine," he said. "Just like before."

"No, that's not it, exactly." I pulled out an old auto-club map yellowed around ragged edges. Creased and creased again from folding and re-folding. Baja Norte on one side. Sur on the other.

I pointed to a spot on the Baja Sur side. "I'm going to need it far down. Somewhere past Todos. With plenty of gas. Maybe a 55-gallon drum or two on board and a pump. And an AK. Maybe four magazines to go with it. I need to tape them."

César whistled again.

"You are headed to Cabo, yes? I forgot. Are you planning on taking on a cartel all by yourself with a single AK? And only dos cuernos de chivos?"

I looked César in the eye. "Not exactly, but I want to be prepared."

César patted the pocket with the money before heading off and only nodded. Years ago, when I ran into him by accident and ended up chartering one of his pangas, he behaved the same way. Money never seemed to be one of his concerns.

"If you need more, I have it," I said.

I finished stacking the upholstery and stretched out on the hard metal in the back of the van. I fell asleep almost immediately. Nervous exhaustion. That, and worrying if my half-assed plan would ever start coming together.

Already I was running late. I would need to make up some time.

FOUR

It **was dark** when César insisted I take the van for a drive to put it through its paces. He was concerned about the added weight on the suspension. Whether the brakes would be affected. I wasn't worried. Down and back, I told him.

"Go, Jim. I'll put some fresh fish on and we can wash it down with cervesa. Mami has some desserts she made for the occasion this afternoon."

How could I say no? True, I paid handsomely for César's help with the van. He did most of the work, though. I was merely a helping hand, doing what I was told. But I was itching to get back on the road. I started out wanting to make a quick trip. I already killed a day getting the van prepared. It put me into my second day.

So much for speedy.

The van turned out to be not so speedy, too. It lurched from side to side passing over dips and bumps on the uneven sand road. In its wake a cloud of dust billowed. I considered turning north, but there was no need to test the van's handling on Ensenada streets. All the miles would be on the peninsula highway—Mexico 1—to the south.

I tested the brakes, gently at first, feeling them out. I jammed down the pedal and the smell of burned brake shoes wafting into the cab said they were overtaxed. With steel plates in the front doors, both rear doors, and the bulkhead behind the front seats, the thing was a tank. I twisted the wheel from side to side. The van wallowed, trying to keep up.

The engine raced to keep the speed at ninety kilometers. That was all right. The limit was 80 on Mexico 1, so I was safe that way. Hell, if I had to, I could cruise all day at 70 and no one would notice in this country. All in all, I was satisfied. César was right to make me take it on a shakedown.

Driving at night on lonely Mexico highways wasn't a good idea. There were more beaters on the road than newer cars and trucks. Lights burned out and people kept driving without them. I couldn't blame them. Everyone had to be somewhere, and a used car was the primary method of transportation. That it didn't have lights or working brakes or the tires were bald didn't matter.

The orange glow on the horizon grew brighter as I neared César's turnoff from the highway. Ensenada's bright lights lay on the horizon. I drew closer, and convinced myself it was a pretty good building-fire in town. Probably downtown, where the construction was older and the old wood frames were dry. A good bonfire would pave the way for needed new construction.

I was maybe a kilometer from the turnoff to César's when I topped a rise. The glow wasn't coming from the city. It was coming from César's. His workshop probably.

He did a lot of welding to secure the armor plate in the van. That had to be it. A spark ignited a rag. Or some stray insulation.

And I believed it, too. That is, until the SUVs made the turn onto the highway and headed north toward Ensenada. I doused my lights and turned the van into one of those invisible beaters I'd been complaining about. I coasted to the side of the road and got into the back.

The extra mags and ammunition for the handgun were where I stashed them before leaving on the test drive. I slipped the automatic between the seat and the center console and floored the gas pedal.

I drew closer and discovered it wasn't the workshop. It was César's home. Or what was left of it. The fire crackled and popped and glowed a brighter orange as stray sections of the interior collapsed and fed the flames.

I didn't need headlights to see the bodies on the ground in front of the house. I recognized two. César and Mami. I tucked the Model 17 into my waistband and checked for a pulse. Nothing. Their dead hands gripped automatics.

Two more bodies were barely visible, illuminated by the bonfire of César's home. I approached. Heard a groan. Kicked a handgun out of the way and picked it up. There was no pulse on the second body. I fired once before wiping the gun clean. I replaced it in a dead man's hand.

César's workshop remained standing, untouched by the blaze. I opened the door and flicked on the lights. His toolbox was open, the way he left it. I slid open the bottom drawer. It was where he stashed the cash I left him. I pocketed what was left and immediately felt guilty for stealing from a dead man.

That lasted about as long as it took to get my ass back to the van and out to the highway. I said a silent thanks to César for chasing me out on the test drive.

I would have waved farewell, but there was no one left to see it.

FIVE

Mexico 1. **The** only road south to La Paz. Past it, Cabo, unless you considered the turnoff at San Pedro onto 19. Paved yet narrow, Mexico 1 ran for a thousand miles from the border. I knew better than to be on it at night. Especially when shoulders on both sides were narrow to non-existent. What shoulder there was disappeared into the night beyond the capability of the van's feeble headlights.

I knew from experience that wasn't good. An errant tire could get sucked into the vacuum and force the heavy van into a rollover—perhaps not a problem given my slow speed, but certainly a problem for righting it. Then there were the animals that came out of the dark, or worse, nowhere. No swerving allowed.

A painted center line could be so faint from wear and tear and heat as to be useless, completely invisible in spots. The only other indicator of both sides of the roadway was where the uneven two halves of the pavement met during construction.

I knew to expect washouts. And then there were the vados. A vado was a cement road crossing filled with rain water. They too could come up out of the dark all of a sudden. If the water laying in them was stale, and chances are it was, the vado would be covered in a slippery morass of green algae. Stopping not recommended. Neither was hitting the brakes trying to stop with nothing but algae for traction.

Topes, or speed bumps, graced the streets of many small highway towns. They were usually unmarked and sat very high. Hitting one at speed would launch the overweight van into the air. If the undercarriage survived the landing that alone would be remarkable.

So what was I doing on a Baja highway at night? Before I could think of even one good reason, headlights flickered in the rearview. I dropped below the crest of a hill and they disappeared. I reached to flip a switch César insisted he install. It turned off my tail lights. That gesture made me the suicide driver of an unlit beater on a beat-up highway to nowhere.

I silently thanked César for wiring up a kill switch for the brake and tail lights, and another for the headlights. Stolen plates for Baja sur completed the deal. If someone was searching for a van with gringo plates, they would be sorely disappointed.

I wondered if the errant headlights in my rearview belonged to the SUV I saw pulling out of César's. If they did, I was hoping they'd be hard-pressed to presume I was the wanted party.

So why was I thinking they would be after me? The only giveaway at César's was what remained of the interior left behind in the shop. The shop wasn't the target. I hoped whoever torched César's and murdered him and his wife hadn't noticed the leftovers from the van fortifications.

SIX

I drove through the night and into the next day. Twenty sweaty, exhausting hours later saw me on the outskirts of La Paz. My down-and-back in three days disappeared out the window and I barely noticed. Mexico time, I used to call it. Seems like it was still around. No matter what you wanted to do, no matter how familiar the job, it always took longer than you figured on.

Never mind that the delays were no one's fault but my own. I managed a catnap or two, or even three somewhere in those last twenty hours. Still, I was exhausted. I parked half a block from the malecón. I yawned before getting out of the stale, dead air in the van. I made for the malecón on foot. Old habits, I figured, but I'd be able to get a taco and a beer, at least.

I walked the length, inhaling the fresh sea air. It wasn't the old malecón I once knew where I watched whales playing in the calm, smooth waters of the bay. It was rebuilt in the not too distant past. It was an even bigger tourist trap now with locals and gabachos mixing it up yet remaining in their separate worlds.

I picked up a couple of fish tacos and a Sol to wash

them down. I found a seat to watch the antics of the gabacho turistas. Pot, meet kettle. I wanted to keep the van in sight, too.

The woman was tall and slender. Her hair was cut in the style of silent movie star Louise Brooks in the movie Pandora's Box. My glance slowed to travel the length of her and ended up at her feet. My tired eyes landed on the brightest white sneakers I ever saw.

I decided she was a lot younger than I first thought. Maybe late teens. Seventeen or eighteen at the most. Immediately I halted my appraisal. A teenager. Too young. Way too young. It had to be exhaustion. I gave my head a shake and my face flushed red with embarrassment.

In one hand she gripped a cell phone. The other held a wad of cash. It occurred to me that whatever she was trying to do, it wasn't going to end well. I waited and watched and remembered to look at the van occasionally, too.

Money. She was trying to change money. I knew because another teenager, a local, stood in front of her, blocking her way as she tried to move past him. His eyes shifted from the phone to the cash and back, as though he couldn't make up his mind. I took a final pull on the beer and got up from the bench. Reluctantly left the remainder of my tacos and beer. I moved toward the girl. Kept a few paces away.

"He'll steal your money or your phone or both and you won't be able to do anything about it," I warned her.

She looked at me and rolled her eyes like I was a

moron not worth the attention. Right away I knew I was right about her age. Red hair framed a freckled face and bright green eyes.

"You better believe it. He'll disappear in a flash. What is it you need?" That broke the ice.

"Money. I'm trying to exchange dollars for pesos," she said.

The local cursed the interruption and pretended to wander off. He didn't go far. I reached into my pocket. His eyes moved to me.

"How much do you need?" I asked the redhead.

Red meticulously counted out a hundred with five twenties. I held out my hand to take it and she flipped it away.

"Show me the cash first," Red insisted. "I wouldn't want you running off with my hundred."

"Don't forget about the phone," I grinned. "You're learning."

She only looked annoyed. I peeled off a thousand from my roll and handed it over. She hesitated before handing over the cash, and followed up with a reluctant thanks.

"No prob. Where are your folks?"

She didn't answer right away. She was busy counting the pesos. "They're around the corner getting something to eat. I'm meeting them there," she said when she was done counting.

"All right. I'll walk with you if you want."

I caught her out giving my shoes the once-over. A horrified look appeared and she looked away in a hurry before dashing off. I wondered what it was about the shoes. Not so fancy. No socks. Maybe they smelled. Van rot from the last twenty-four hours. Hell, her own were the Nike Air Force variety. I was wearing the exact same thing. Black as the night. Hers were whiter than white.

It was obvious Red didn't want my help, so I went and took a seat behind the coffee shop counter, facing the street. It would give me time to duck if I saw anything suspicious. Before the lead started flying. I recognized a couple of uniforms in the café and no one beyond wait staff. That alone caused me to become even more uneasy.

I drank my coffee fast. Paid fast. Crossed the street to my now armor-plated beater I bought in a hurry in San Diego. Cursed out loud for forgetting my beer and tacos on the bench. I unlocked the door to get into the van and then thought better of it while I went to look for a phone card. I was pretty sure I'd call Maddie. Eventually.

Through the tienda's window I caught sight of the girl climbing into the unlocked van's driver door. I cursed again at my forgetfulness. A slim pair of legs ending in a bony rear end polished the windshield from the inside before disappearing over the armor plating. I went back for another coffee and laid out the cash at the counter before making for the van.

"I got us coffee. You want one?" I asked. I wasn't sure if you took cream and sugar, so I grabbed a handful, just in case."

Silence. There was nothing. Not a sound. No nervous breathing. No ruffle or flutter of clothes or backpack. Either she was practiced or so scared she couldn't move.

I climbed in and slammed the door shut. "You planning on slitting my throat from back there?" I waited her out.

"No."

One word. So far. I considered it a success. She stood up to look at me. I wasn't so pretty in the mirror with my own reflection staring back. Not that I ever thought I was. I rubbed at my chin. Scraped stubble. More than that. I had near to a full beard in progress.

"I'll dump the coffee if you don't want it," I said.

"Fine."

"Fine," I repeated. "Fine you want the coffee, or fine you don't?"

She sighed at my bad joke.

"You better climb in front. If you stay back there, you'll make me nervous. I don't like being nervous."

Red stammered something I couldn't make out. Attempted to get in the front the same way she climbed into the back. It didn't work for her, especially with me taking up a seat.

"Why don't you try throwing a leg over like it's a fence. It works better. It's more graceful, too."

The girl settled into the seat with a satisfied sigh and reached for the coffee.

"Where are you headed that you need so many pesos?"

"Cabo San Lucas. You?"

"Down the road a piece." It was nobody's business where I was going.

"Can I come with you?" she asked, out of nowhere.

So much for her folks getting a bite at that restaurant.

Great. All I needed. An underage girl tagging along. A babysitter I was not. And in any event, who the hell did she think she was? I had no time for this. I was dedicated to picking up my cash and scurrying north across the border as fast as I could. Already I was behind schedule.

"I don't think that would be a good idea. Where are your parents really?"

"Back home."

Two word answers. I kept the questions the same. "Where's that?"

"Florida," she said.

I didn't see any way out of babysitting duties after that. I offered my hand. "I'm Jim Nash." She didn't take it.

"I'm Anya."

It sounded like Anna. I didn't ask, because I didn't care. She wouldn't be around long enough. I pulled into traffic and made for the highway with my hitch-hiker in the seat beside me. She busied herself with sipping at her coffee while ignoring me by looking out the side window. We were hardly moving with the traffic yet.

SEVEN

Babysitting wasn't part of the plan. Neither was the transmission that clunked into gear. I steered the van away from the malecón. It wallowed into the corners. For something to do I opened the door and slammed it shut. Nothing. She didn't even twitch.

"Where did you say you were headed?" I asked. Just in case Red changed her mind between then and now. Like that restaurant her parents were supposedly sitting down to eat but weren't.

"Cabo San Lucas." She hesitated. "What about you?"

"What about me, what?"

"Where are you headed?"

"I already told you. Down the road a piece." I could dump her at Todos Santos. Or anywhere, for that matter.

"Fine."

That word again. She put her feet up on the dash and pushed back into the seat. The shoes were almost blinding. The transmission clunked again and the engine groaned and we were off.

"Does this thing have a radio?"

"What's a radio?" She didn't see my humor.

"What happened to your phone?" I hadn't seen it

since she climbed in.

"It's with my backpack."

I reached for the radio and turned it on. "See if you can find a station."

She fiddled with the buttons. Nothing came up. A hand smacked the dash.

"You could try your foot, too."

A tinny sound came through. Mexican music. Probably hits. I had no idea. "All right. Well, you were successful."

Now what? I still had no room for anyone on this fly-by-night trip down the Baja. I was delayed at César's. Now the man and his wife were both dead, thanks to me. I had planned on doing this trip in one day. Or one night. That was done for. The morning was going fast.

"I have a place I need to stop at to check travel arrangements. It's down the road a bit."

That was true. The last thing I asked César for was a go-fast panga. I remembered he thought I was being overly cautious. The man didn't know I would be coming home with over a half a million dollars. In cash. I didn't want to explain.

"So I guess that means you're taking me with you," she said.

With La Paz in the rearview I turned onto the main road that took us south to the turnoff for Todos. I would make it before dark. It would be easy to convince the girl it was my final destination.

EIGHT

The military checkpoint came up just before the highway split into the turnoff for Todos Santos. They could cover two highways for the price of one. I pulled to the side of the road.

Anya glanced in my direction. It was a nervous look. "Why are we stopping?"

I needed to settle some things before we went on. "We're coming up to a checkpoint. You can see it just ahead of us."

Anya shifted in the bucket seat. Nerves, probably.

"There'll be men with guns. Mexican troops. I need to see some ID." She had to have a passport. She needed one to get home.

Anya turned to reach into the back. She dragged her backpack over the steel plate. Fished in it. Came up with a wallet. Flashed a driver's license.

"Hand it over."

She passed me her wallet. I studied it. Read the name. Checked the birth date. "Number one, this isn't a real Florida license. Number two, you're not twenty-one."

"I am too." Indignant that I would question the veracity of her proof.

"No, you're not. I'm from Florida, and I have a Florida license. It doesn't look anything like that. Good try, though."

"Fine." She crossed her arms and turned away to look out the window. "I guess you'll be letting me out, then."

It was a pretty good performance, but for the fact we had to pass through the checkpoint to get anywhere. And I sure as hell wasn't about letting the girl out in the middle of nowhere into a miscellaneous collection of Mexican troops. "I'm still waiting."

"Fine."

Anya seemed to like that word. A lot. She rummaged through her backpack. It was a good delaying tactic, but still. Eventually a hand came out holding a passport. I made a grab for it. Flipped it open. Examined the picture. Looked at her. Looked back at the passport.

"Ah. You have a birthday coming up in a couple of days. Lucky you."

She'd be celebrating on the side of the road all by herself if I had anything to do with it. That wasn't the immediate problem, though.

"Here's the deal. Pay attention."

Apparently, she already was, because she looked across at me. Stared is more like it. Scared more like it, too. Her first trip to Mexico.

"You're a minor. I could be in trouble if someone thinks we're not related. You are now my step-daughter. Get it? Nod and say yes. And let me see your passport again, Anya."

I read the name again. Anya Quinn. An Irish name if

ever there was one. "What are we, dear?"

She frowned. "You're my step-dad. Jim Nash."

So she was paying attention when I told her my name. "That's my girl. And don't you forget it for a minute, Anya Quinn."

"Do we have to stop?"

She was worried. I braked behind the car at the end of the short line. It was time to pass on a lesson in Mexican diplomacy. "Take a look around. Do you see anything out of the ordinary?"

"You mean besides the men with guns?" she asked?

"Yes. Do you notice any fortifications of any kind? Ever watch a war movie?"

"Yeah, no."

Very well then. "Allow me to point out a couple of positions to you. Do you see the raised mound with the slit?"

"You mean the building over there?" She pointed.

To the untrained eye, that's all there was to see. I pointed in the opposite direction. She looked. There was no sign of recognition until she saw what she thought I was pointing at."

"Ohh. That little mound of dirt. There's a gun pointing out." She got it.

"Yup. There's another one on the other side. See it?"

She recognized the second gun nest and nodded excitedly. Except this wasn't a quiz show. "That's why you don't run a checkpoint. Those machine gun nests might be manned. They might not. Don't take the chance. In any case, where would you escape to? The road only runs north and south. They've got you covered."

"What are they looking for at the checkpoint?"

"Drugs. Guns and ammunition. Firearms aren't allowed to be brought into the country by anyone. Except the cartels, of course."

"I don't care about them." Exasperated, Anya sat back, put her feet up on the dash, and crossed her ankles. "Okay. I'm ready, step-dad."

"There's one more thing."

She sighed, exasperated. "What now?"

"Have you got any drugs? I don't want to end up in a Mexican prison on account of a stranger I'm doing a favor. Neither do you. In any case, your ride would be a lot worse than mine."

"I don't do drugs," Anya said.

Great. I was the baby-sitter I didn't want to be. Todos Santos and freedom couldn't come fast enough.

NINE

It wasn't soon enough when I passed the highway sign announcing Todos Santos. In a couple of minutes I was downtown in the small tourist town. I pulled to the side of the street and parked. "I'll let you out here. I'm going to take a break and get something to eat."

Anya leaned into the back and dragged her backpack over the steel plate. She got out and closed the door. Her head came partway in the window. "Okay, well, I guess I'll be seeing you. Thanks for the ride this far."

She moved to step away and then turned back. She didn't want to leave. I couldn't help her there. "And thanks for the coffee. I take cream and sugar," she admitted.

It was obvious she wanted to ask if I was going farther. As if I didn't have enough baggage. "You're welcome. So long." There were too many good-byes in my life. So long seemed to say it better anyway. "Be safe, Anya."

"I will. Thanks again." She waved in that way that said she didn't want to leave. Hesitated. A nervous smile took over her face. She remained beside the van, reluctant to walk away. I contemplated what I'd do if she ended up back in the van while I was out of sight eating. I really didn't want to be anyone's babysitter. I had a job to do. One that needed to get done. Down and back. That's what I told myself. Down and back as fast as I could go.

Anya walked off, finally. Head down. She slowed and turned to look back, like a puppy, before finally shouldering her bag. She waved again and continued walking. I figured she'd catch a ride at the south end of town and be long gone by the time I had a beer and ate and got back on the road.

Who wouldn't stop for a good-looking American girl?

The hot sun felt like it was burning holes in my damp, sweaty clothes. I eavesdropped on too many Americanos talking about rumors of cartel bloodshed on the border with Mexico. How the Mexican police always seemed to arrive late and outgunned. How there had been twenty-five or thirty thousand drug-related murders in the past year alone.

Well no shit, Sherlock. It was all about the drugs. And the insatiable market for the poison back home. Hell, that was why I was down here now. Why I had an armor-plated van. Why I'd picked up mags and ammo to outfit an army.

I wasn't back on the road that long when the damned girl appeared hitching outside my turnoff south of Todos. I pulled up beside her before I noticed the dog cradled in her arms. She put him on the ground and approached, throwing a toothy smile in my direction.

Shit. Now what? I had somewhere I needed to be, and it wasn't anywhere near her. Dog or not. Hell, she even had water for him. "Who's your friend?"

I picked her up on the way out of town. She wouldn't go back. She kept following me.

"Yeah, well, you gave her water, didn't you?"

"Of course. She was thirsty. What else could I do?"

Well, you could have let her die by the side of the road like a dog. I didn't say it, of course. I was reminded of a road trip down here where I counted daily miles— Mexican kilometers, if you must—by the carcasses of dead dogs I passed on the side of the road.

TEN

Anya stood in front of me, protective shoulders hunched forward, cradling the dog in her arms. It was busy twisting its head, trying to lick the girl's face as Anya pressed her cheek to the dog.

"Do you have to bring that thing?"

She looked at me like I just offered to shoot it. "Yes. I have to bring the dog."

"All right then. Get in and close the door."

"Does that mean you're going to take me to Cabo San Lucas?"

"It's Cabo," I told her. "Everyone calls it Cabo."

"Fine. Are you going to take me to Cabo?"

"Yes," I finally admitted. "Happy now?"

The struggling dog finally succeeded in licking the girl's face. Anya giggled. Satisfied, the dog looked over at me, probably wondering if it could make me giggle, too. There wasn't much chance of that. All the dog succeeded in doing was making me even more grumpy. A dog and a hitchhiker. I needed my head examined.

"What are you going to call it?"

"Oreo."

Oreo? Who the hell names a dog after a cookie? He was

black and white though. Maybe that was it. "How do you know what his name is?"

"I don't. She's a girl, though. I checked."

Hitchhikers and dogs. Whatever. South of Todos I turned off the highway onto the dirt road and climbed the slight hill to a dune buggy business. It had to be popular, judging by what was in the parking lot. Moneyed gabachos with too much time on their hands pretending to be on a Baja 500 for half a day, getting drunk, and suffering through a bad sunburn.

Anya looked across the seat at me. "I thought—"

"You didn't think. You didn't ask. Now do what I tell you or you can get out right now."

To make my point, I was the one to get out. I slammed the door and walked past the parked cars, trucks and Baja buggies. Some of the buggies were on trailers. Most weren't. The business had to be a going concern. Gabacho license plates were everywhere.

César had given me a name. At the counter I asked for Luz. Pronounced it Loos, as it should be. The query caused a bit of a commotion when the person I asked disappeared for what seemed like forever. I wandered around the sales floor pretending to admire the Baja buggy hardware.

"Señor Jim?"

It was the boy from behind the counter. "Si."

"When Luz heard you were in Todos she left for the beach. You can find her there."

"Gracias."

I wondered what I'd find waiting on the beach. I started

out coasting down a steep bank onto a dry riverbed. A cloud of dust kicked up behind the overweight van as I eased pressure on the gas pedal, concerned it would get bogged down in the soft, loose sand. It bobbed and weaved on its own as I struggled to make progress.

"Where are we going?"

I looked across at Anya. She appeared nervous. She was hugging the dog tight. It was obvious she wanted to be somewhere else rather than trapped in a van with a rando madman who picked her up a second time. "You want to go to Cabo?"

"I-I-I—" she stammered.

Of course she did. "We're going to Cabo and we're doing it my way." That seemed to quiet her. Sorted, finally.

I spotted the ATV before I saw the person squatting beside it, waiting out of sight in the shade. The girl must have heard the van laboring over the sand, because she stood up.

"What's she wearing?" Anya asked. "What's that across her shoulders?"

"I'm not positive from here, but I'm guessing it's the AK I ordered."

"AK? What's an AK?" Anya wanted to know.

I didn't answer. She could figure it out for herself. Meanwhile, I halted the van beside the solitary person on the beach. It had to be Luz. She was fourteen. Sixteen, tops. Maybe.

"Señor Jim?"

I hadn't been called that for a while. "Si, Luz. I'm señor Jim."

"I have for you everything César ordered. He asked me to treat you just as I would treat him."

That was kind of César. I promised myself I would leave him a little extra when I passed by on the way home. Then I remembered that wouldn't be happening.

Anya leaned over, stuck me with a bony elbow, and whispered. "She can't be more than thirteen or fourteen, señor Jim."

It distracted me from my thoughts. "You're probably right," I agreed.

Anya clutched the dog tight with one arm and exited the van. Oreo barked and squirmed.

"You found my dog!" Luz exclaimed. "Where was she?"

Anya looked from me to the girl, knowing she was excited to see her dog again. I wondered if she wanted me to convince Luz to let her take Oreo with us.

"Don't look at me. You dug this hole all by yourself."

Luz handed over the AK and a heavy canvas bag before taking the dog from Anya. I slung the AK over my shoulder and handed the ammo bag to Anya. "Put that in the panga. I'll be along in a minute." She didn't look real happy to be here. I could tell by the way she eyed the AK Luz handed over.

"You better get out of that dress." When had she changed? She was wearing cargo shorts in La Paz. "You're going to need long pants and a long-sleeved shirt," I told her. "A bandana wouldn't hurt. And a cap. If you have sunscreen put it on all the bare parts. All of them."

"Yes master."

I should have smacked her right then. Instead I went to

the van to retrieve her backpack. "Change. You better dig out your sunglasses too. We've got a long way to go over lots of open water."

I turned my back and my eyes caught a flash of light. I made sure to turn my head slowly, roaming over the dry-land horizon. A dune buggy sat exposed on the high bank of the dry river bed. Nothing unusual about that. The area was a playground for those things. I didn't see any people.

"Do not worry, señor Jim. They are with me."

"Luz. We need to talk." I led her to her dune buggy and told her about her friend, César, and his helping me both times. Explained what I found when I tried to return to his place after test driving the van.

She wasn't shocked. "This is Mexico. It happens all the time now, to everyone" she said. "I will take your van and store it in a safe place until you and the girl come back, señor Jim."

I didn't ask Luz how she would know when we came back. I left that up to her.

ELEVEN

I waited for Anya to climb aboard the panga in her long pants and short-sleeved shirt, pleased she had taken most of my advice. She had even covered her head with a ball cap. Sunglasses shaded her eyes. "You won't be sorry," I told her.

She frowned and explored the cramped cockpit while Luz and I pushed the heavy panga off the sand. It floated free and I climbed aboard and joined Anya. Luz stood and waved before making for the van. I waited while she backed it around and headed up the dry riverbed through a lingering cloud of dust.

The panga bobbed in the light swell thanks to the lack of wind. That wasn't usual from my memory. I dropped the triple engines into the water, fired her up, and eased into reverse before turning and aiming it offshore. I idled out a hundred yards and shut down.

"I told you to put on a long-sleeve shirt. We have quite a distance to go to get to Cabo. We'll be on the water for hours. Do you want to burn your skin off, or do you want to be as comfortable as possible when we get there?"

Anya gave me another dirty look. I was getting

popular that way. Her cap was too loose. I dug in my bag. "Here. Wear it. Put a bandana around your neck, too. It'll help keep the sun off. And torque down the hat. It's going to be windy. In the meantime, come up here."

I didn't want to give her time to think about the circumstance she found herself in. She approached reluctantly. I couldn't blame her. I was being hard on her. "Have you ever piloted a boat?"

She shook her head.

"Well, in that case, you're going to learn." I moved away from the controls. "Stand like I was standing. Put the back of your legs against the edge of the seat bottom. Do it the same way I was doing it."

She positioned herself at the helm and stood there. I didn't make her wait.

"The only thing I'm not familiar with is this modern GPS nav screen. Do you think you can master it between now and Cabo?"

She scrunched down and mumbled something before going for her phone. In five minutes she had the image on her phone and was reading about the GPS navigation system and its controls. "I think I've got it. Yes."

She reached to switch it on. The screen lit beneath the hood. It was difficult to see at first. She punched a button. "That marked our present position. If you want to come here, just hit it and the boat will home on it. Okay?"

I nodded. It would only do that if the controls were

tied into the GPS.

"From what I read we can set markers all along the way to Cabo. You know, for when you tell the GPS to backtrack on your original course. Like I said, it will take us to the beach we just left."

"Good. You can show me when we get to sea. Start her up."

She looked at me like she wanted the security blanket of the dog to hold onto. "You heard me. Start her up."

She moved to turn the key.

"Wait. Did you check the position of the engines?" I pulled them out of the water with the electric motor. "If you start them now and advance the throttles, all they'll do is make a lot of noise and overheat." I pointed. "There's the lever. Hit it."

Three engines whined their way into the water. Anya hit the starter and they settled into a purr.

"That's the sound you want to hear. Remember it. The throttles are on the transom by your right hand."

She hit it so hard I flew straight back. My arms flailed. I stumbled against the engines. They kept me from going overboard. I worked my way back to the cockpit. "Take us south using the compass. See it there? Keep our position in sight on the GPS. We want to try and stay in shallow water."

She nodded and kept silent as she concentrated on piloting the go-fast panga. Somehow, César had arranged for a brand-new boat, outfitted with all the gear a go-fast would need to smuggle drugs. I really did owe him. Dead or alive.

I gave Anya ten minutes at the controls before I motioned to her to slow down. She pulled back the throttles to idle. The bow crashed into the water and the boat slowed fast.

"What's wrong?" she asked. She didn't look happy. "What did I screw up?"

TWELVE

There was nothing wrong. It was time for a sailing lesson. "I've never seen anyone look so disappointed. All ahead one-third and take a gentle angle into shore," I told her.

"Aye Captain." She looked across at me and rolled her eyes, but she did as she was told. She eased the wheel toward shore. We were getting close. She looked at me again. The wheel stayed steady and she throttled back to idle.

"See how the water changes color? It gets lighter the closer we get to shore."

She nodded and looked and nodded again. "Oh yeah. I do see what you mean."

"Sand bottom. Beach. Bikinis. Suntanning women. And men."

"I hope the men aren't in—"

I didn't give her a chance. "The old men are wearing speedos."

"Oh crap." Anya covered her eyes with a hand and peeked out between splayed fingers. "But yeah, I see what you mean."

"What does it tell you about what's beneath the

panga?" I asked, to reinforce the lesson.

"The water is getting shallow."

"That's right. Now take a look behind us."

She turned to look. We were drifting to a point where we'd soon be aground. "Sand. Sand in the water. The propellers—" She throttled up just a bit and behind us the water churned into a sandy cloud.

"That's right. You better take her out a bit. Not too far. Just enough to make sure we're not churning sand. See that gauge?" I tapped it. "That's a depth finder. It tells you how much water is beneath the panga. It points straight down. Not ahead."

"It's only for right under the boat."

"The panga. That's right."

Anya fiddled with the GPS, punching buttons and marking our spot. A chart came up showing the offshore contours. She pointed to it and looked pleased. "This shows what's ahead."

"Yes it does." I was secretly pleased. In a week I would never have learned this system.

She beamed at me, proud of what she was able to do with the electronic chart. I grinned back. This one wasn't a slouch in the smart department.

"Good for you. I would never have been able to do that."

"You'd find it if there was a manual. Or if you had a phone to look it up. Why don't you have one?"

I ignored the question. "Maybe. But there's no manual. And you're the one with the phone."

My eyes scanned across the bow. "What's coming up?"

She looked ahead, confused. It lasted for only a moment. "Darker water."

"That's right. And what does that mean?"

She pointed to shore at the rocky outcrop that went on for a bit of distance. "We can hug the shore there."

"Then do it."

She punched in a marker for where we were, and when we arrived close in to shore, she hit another one. When we passed the outcrop, she hit another marker. It was enough to impress me.

I had a new captain. Maybe even an Admiral.

THIRTEEN

Anya's abilities with the navigation system impressed me. She turned out to be a quick study. She was pretty proud of herself, too. I asked for her phone and snapped a quick photo. I took another one when she turned to look at me with a huge, shit-eating grin pasted on her face. I couldn't blame her. She was the captain. I was a lowly first mate, but I had more training in mind beyond reading the depth.

Still grinning, she gestured ashore at water cascading down a rocky cliff face. "Is that fresh water?"

"It is. Do you have something in mind?" I wanted to know.

"Well, I could use a bath. You could, too. And I need to wash some clothes."

"Are you telling me I smell?"

"Yeah, no. I'm saying you reek to high heaven. And even heaven can't help you now."

Smartass eased back the triple throttles. The panga slowed instantly and collapsed on its bottom. She steered for shore, mindful of the panga's speed.. Her eyes roamed from the depth finder to the chart showing on the screen and back to shore. I did the same.

"How much farther do you think I should go?" she asked.

"The tide looks to be out. We're safe to get a little closer. When it comes in, we'll float higher. But that won't be for hours."

"All righty then, we're here," she announced. She shut down the engines. I went up front to drop anchor. The motor whined and the engines came out of the water.

"I'm going to take the AK. Are you okay with that?"

If she said no, it wouldn't matter in the slightest. The AK was coming with us, and she'd be the one carrying it. I didn't let on about that.

"Sure. Why not? Are you expecting trouble?"

"Not really," I said, "but this is Mexico. It's best to not be certain of anything." I jumped into the water and sank waist-deep. "We probably could have come in closer."

"I can bring it in."

She was eager to please. "Not unless you raise the anchor. We're good here."

She took the hint and handed me the ammo bag and my backpack. I waded ashore and deposited both on the beach before going back. She handed over her backpack before putting a leg over the gunnel.

"Not so fast, Captain. Aren't you forgetting something?"

She appeared confused. Her head turned to check

the panga from bow to stern. "What?"

"The AK."

"You want me to carry that?"

"Yes. I want you to carry that," I insisted. "How about it?"

"All right. If you say so."

I waited while she wrestled with the strap before handing it down to me. She eased herself into the water without complaining. I handed the rifle back.

"If it gets wet, you'll pay. Big time." Anya hoisted the AK over her head with arms extended.

"That's my girl."

She grinned and all of a sudden looked serious. "This thing is heavy."

"Yeah, almost eight pounds worth empty. It doesn't get any lighter, either."

Halfway to shore she looked back and saw me climbing into the boat.

"If you leave me here—" She was trying not to sound panicky. It wasn't working.

"I'd be long gone if I was going to do that. I'm collecting the key." I held it up for her to see.

I caught up and we made our way to a freshwater pool fed by a small stream rushing down the rock outcrop. "You have a sharp eye. You did good."

Anya beamed at me. She was proud of herself, too. "Thank you. Now turn around. I'm jumping into the pool. Don't look."

"Anya—" Already her jeans were down around her knees.

"Shut up. Turn around. Don't look."

I did as I was told and waited for the splash and the all-clear. By the time she called out, she was already soaping and scrubbing clothes. By the look of it, it was everything she owned.

"You know you're going to have to climb out of that pond to get dressed, right? You haven't left yourself anything to wear."

"Don't worry about me. Worry about you. You still aren't doing your laundry, mister. And I for one am tired of smelling you."

Cripes, was the van so bad even I didn't notice? "Okay, okay, you guilted me enough. Now it's time you closed your eyes."

I stripped down, jumped in, and surfaced. The water was fresh and cool. Just what I needed. "Soap. Where's the soap?"

She tossed the bar. It slipped from my one-handed catch and splashed out of sight. By the time I found it and surfaced, Anya was out of the water and tying her bikini. She mimed holding her nose as she unzipped my backpack and dumped everything onto the sand. She used both hands to throw my clothes into the water.

"Don't come out until everything is squeaky clean, mister."

I saluted. "Aye, Captain."

She wrung out her clothes and hung them on the bushes surrounding the pool. I called to her and laughed. "Do you do ironing too?"

"Not today. I'm going for a walk to dry off. Call out when you're ready to leave."

Wet clothes fluttered on branches in the strong breeze off the ocean.

FOURTEEN

I didn't have to call out. Anya scrambled toward the clothes spread out on the brush. She rushed, first one foot, then another as she struggled to don her pants. Her foot caught on the belt and she fell over, cursing the entire time. "There's someone coming. There's someone coming."

I already knew. A Mexican patrol boat was holding abeam our panga. Two crew members were taking a look through binoculars. "Anya. I need you to do me a favor please."

She was still trying to get a second leg into her long pants, unsuccessfully, as she stumbled and fell again.

"Please don't get dressed. And throw me a pair of shorts, please. Hurry."

"What? Why?"

"They're checking you out. Take a look for yourself. They're not looking at me. I need them to be checking you out. I want them to think we're on a getaway. Please?"

She did as I asked, but not before the Fine I knew to be coming. She stood facing the patrol boat, hands on hips, looking indignant before finally smiling and waving a greeting. The men were satisfied. The boat advanced throttles and turned away to head out to sea.

"Thanks for doing that."

"Why? Why did you ask me?"

"Well, now I know for sure they patrol the area. If they see us again, they're more likely to ignore us. If they don't, they have you to look at and think I'm a lucky son of a gun." I held up my hands before she could respond.

"I know. I know. It's sexist. And you're still underage. But I have a job to do, and you're part of it now, whether you like it or not. I'm responsible for your safety the only way I know how."

It took the fun out of our brief escape, but I had to make her understand. It was the only way to do it. I didn't want her to take it personally. I cursed silently for bringing her on this madcap adventure I found myself on. It was time to get down to business before she thought I was using her. Then I considered for a moment and knew I was using her.

"Anya?"

"What do you want now? The patrol boat is gone." She was fed up.

"I need to show you something."

"It better not be a dick pic." She threw me a disgusted look.

"Damn, woman. Cut me some slack." I turned bright pink and she laughed so hard at my embarrassment I thought she'd fall down. In fact, she almost did. I grabbed one of my shirts from the bush and spread it on the beach. I sat the AK on top of it. Anything to change the subject.

"This is a Russian AK." I racked and cleared. "Where

are you going now?" She was up and walking away. Teenagers. They came with the attention span of a—

"I'm going to the panga. There's food in that cooler Luz left for us. If we're lucky the ice is still good. I'll be right back."

She pulled her shirt up and waded to the panga. She offloaded the cooler and floated it to shore. She popped the lid. Beer and plenty of water were ice cold and the sandwiches were fresh. We dug in and ate like it was our last meal. In between bites I went over the AK.

"Now as I was saying. This is an AK, also known as the African credit card. Every banana republic in the world is ruled by this rifle. If you watch television news, the images of firearms are almost all of this particular rifle."

She took a swallow of water.

"Except in Mexico. Here it's all about American firearms. The cartels are the only outfits permitted by the government to own firearms."

It was a joke, except it wasn't. The only people who weren't allowed to own firearms were the ordinary Mexican citizens. They were helpless in the face of the cartels' mass murder of civilians.

"And you're telling me this because?"

I reached into the bag and handed off an empty mag. "Because it's going to be your job to load this magazine. Get familiar with it."

She didn't hesitate to pick it up, which surprised me. After I demonstrated how it was done, she hummed and fumbled a time or two before happily feeding rounds into each of the magazines.

"Did you happen to notice any duct tape on the panga?

Anya fished in the cooler and came up with a roll of the gray tape in a plastic bag. Luz thought of everything.

"Excellent."

"What's the tape for?" she wanted to know.

"To tape the mags. They're sometimes called banana clips when they're taped. Or jungle clips. Technically, they're still magazines. And technically they're still called jungle clips."

"Why?"

"The standard AK magazine is 30 rounds. Taping two magazines together will give you 60 rounds with a minimum of fuss."

She regarded me like I was crazy. "Moi? What do you mean, me? Did I hear that right? Surely you jest, oh admiral of the fleet."

I chuckled anyway. "No. I'm not jesting. And keep busy. You have four more to do."

The brass jingled in the ammo bag every time she reached in, until it was empty.

"These things are heavy." She plopped the last loaded magazine on the shirt and looked too pleased with herself.

"Yes they are. Now pass them over. I need to check your handiwork."

FIFTEEN

The ocean wind was beginning to pick up. The fresh breeze rustled the bushes surrounding the freshwater pond. Our clothes billowed. They wouldn't be getting any drier. I stood up and gathered everything. Immediately Anya began folding.

"Your mother must like you."

"So far. My dad does, too."

"Good to hear. Now you need to get into your clothes. The long pants and shirt. You're starting to burn."

I had enough of the bikini. And I was too polite to check out a teenager. It just wasn't right. "Here. Turn around before you put that shirt on."

Her entire body was covered in freckles. A typical redhead. She'd burn in an instant. I spread suntan oil on her shoulders and the shirt went on overtop.

"Thanks." She finished the job before handing over the oil. I covered my face and neck before she took it and did the same to my shoulders.

"Now that you're presentable, what's a nice girl like you doing in a place like this?"

She pretended to think for a minute. She was too

easy to read. "Hmm. Well now. Some old guy in La Paz tried to pick me up—" She couldn't help grinning.

"Hey now yourself, Captain. I can reduce your rank any time I want. Oh, and you climbed into my van uninvited. How soon we forget."

Anya switched to serious. "My sister went missing. Now she's found. What can I say? I need a ride to Cabo to catch a flight home."

"That's it? That's why you sneaked into my van on the La Paz malecón?"

"That's all there is to the crime. What are you doing down here?" she asked.

Yeah, that wasn't a question I wanted to answer any time soon. "There's something I need to pick up. I need to bring it home."

She raised an eyebrow. "Don't tell me it's drugs."

"All right, I won't tell you it's drugs. And it isn't, just so you know," I insisted.

She nodded, but I could tell she was thinking. She didn't believe me. "It must be important. What is it?"

"You don't need to know. Maybe later." Maybe later when she was on the plane to home and I was in the panga headed north. Which meant never in my universe. I picked up the AK and racked it to check it was clear. Depressed the tab on the magazine. Tipped it onto the shirt.

"One magazine left for you to fill. What's left in the bag?"

Anya slid out a box and opened it. They were

tracer rounds. I knew by the tips. "Okay, you aren't going to like me any more."

I made her wait before I went on. She could tell something was up.

"Didn't I do it right? I did it the way you showed me."

"You did just fine. But you have to unload the magazines and redo them—" I began.

"But why?"

I opened the tin and held up a round. "Because of these. They're tracers. Unload the magazines and reload them. Every five rounds, throw in one of these."

She grumbled and groaned and began slipping the rounds out of the magazines. When she finished she began counting groups of six including the orange-tipped tracers.

"What's a tracer?"

It took her long enough to ask. She went back to counting. I waited until she finished loading the first six rounds before interrupting.

"In simple terms, a tracer round lights a trail so the shooter can see if he's getting close to the target."

"That's why you need one every five?"

"Exactly. You're learning."

"Yeah. I'm learning something I hope I'll never have to use back home."

"When you go back to school and someone asks you what you did on your summer vacation, you'll have a story to tell."

She halted her work mid-way through a magazine. "That is so high school. I'm headed to art school. And dammit, I lost count."

I left her to finish and went looking for a target. What was the sense of having a firearm if I couldn't fire it?

SIXTEEN

The wind off the Pacific was growing stronger and turning much cooler. The refreshing break in the shallow warmth of the freshwater pool was behind us. I left Anya to her magazines and walked inland. I wanted a sheltered spot where I could sight in the AK. In ten minutes I was back with Anya. She held up the last of the magazines and waved it at me. "Finished," she called, obviously proud of her handiwork.

"Good job. Bring the AK and a magazine and follow me."

She stood up and slung the ammo bag over a shoulder. She picked up the rifle and didn't seem to know what to do with it. She hefted it. Felt the weight. Wrestled with the strap. Managed to keep the muzzle pointed at the ground.

"Uhh, Jim—?"

She passed the test. "Hand it over." I remained a step away. Waited for her to hold it out.

"It's heavy. Did you say eight pounds? That's without the loaded magazine, right? You didn't say."

So she was paying attention. Good. "Yeah, about eight when it's not loaded. Here's what you need to do before you do anything else. With any firearm." I didn't take the proffered weapon.

"Make sure there's no magazine hanging off of it. That's number one."

"Well that's pretty basic," she insisted.

"Yeah. For me. You need to be reminded. Forever."

"Fine."

There was that word again. I grinned. With her hands full of AK she couldn't put them on her hips, bend a knee and tap a toe to pretend impatience. I covered her hands with mine and tilted the weapon to show her the operating handle.

"Pull back on the handle I just showed you. If there's a live round—or a dead one—in the chamber, that will clear it."

She fumbled with the weapon and settled the rifle on her shoulder like a toy soldier before pulling back the handle.

"Now take it off your shoulder and do it right." That didn't go over well. "Wait. We're not finished yet. Don't get impatient. It's a weapon, not a boyfriend."

She looked at me like I was nuts. "How do you know I like boys?"

I turned it around immediately. "It's not a girlfriend, either."

"I like boys."

"Good for you, because the boys are sure going to like you. Now look in the chamber that's open. Is there a round still in it?"

She blushed crimson before answering. "Nope. All

clear."

"Good. Now point the muzzle—that's the end the bullet comes out—in the air. Be sure you're not pointing it at anything you want to kill—"

"Does that mean you?" she interrupted.

I hesitated, regarding her seriously before I went on. "That definitely means me. You can kill me after I get you to Cabo to board your plane. Now pull the trigger. That will close the action, and you can be certain you won't shoot anyone, including yourself."

Anya pulled the trigger. The action slid and the AK snapped closed.

"Excellent," I told her. "When I join the mercs, I want you as my backup."

"Mercs?"

"Mercenaries. Paid fighters. Usually found trying to overthrow dictators in African countries and failing miserably when they get caught out. They get caught and captured because they're all a bunch of liars and thieves and double-crossers with no scruples whatsoever."

"Tell me how you really feel."

"In a minute. Now that we have that settled and your firearm is secure, throw it across your back and I'll adjust the strap for you."

She wrestled with the AK. Made several attempts to get it across her back.

"Put it on like you did the ammo bag. Like a shoulder bag, but let it hang on the opposite side of you."

A light went on. "Ohh. Like this, you mean." She passed the strap over her head and it settled on her opposite shoulder. I grabbed the tabs and shortened the strap. It fit perfectly. Too perfect, maybe. She wasn't wearing a bra.

It was my turn to blush.

SEVENTEEN

I walked us inland. We got our feet wet crossing the freshwater stream and the narrow green belt it provided. The desert presented itself as a vast brown expanse. Plenty of brush would be green when it rained. Now it was only a dirty, dusty brown. It was hot inland, away from the ocean. Anya struggled with the AK and the ammo bag. Sweat covered both of us.

"Well Anya, you did say you wanted a ride. Look at you now."

She halted and wiped perspiration from her forehead and eyes with her shirt. "How much farther?"

I cut her some slack and halted. "Right here is good. Hand over the AK."

Relieved, she sighed and slipped it off her back. "That thing gets heavy, doesn't it? How do kids walk around with one of those in Africa?"

"Practice makes perfect. Now pay attention and you'll be an old pro in no time."

"Thanks. I think." She made sure not to point the muzzle at me. I guessed she didn't want to shoot me. Yet. I'd see how it went from here.

"Hand me the magazine."

She reached into the bag and pulled it out. "These are heavy too."

"Yeah, now picture it hanging off the rifle. Picture two, taped, and try to imagine how much heavier it would be. Do you think you can handle it?"

I showed her how to fit the magazine. How to release it. How to fit it again. I made her practice, and she moaned and groaned but she wouldn't quit. Satisfied, I told her to keep it inserted. "Now heft it to your shoulder. Like you were going to fire it."

I got behind her. Reached around. Supported the AK as she wrestled with it, trying to lift it. I relaxed and allowed her to wrestle with it.

"It's so darned heavy, Jim. I don't think I can." She shifted her weight, struggling to stay balanced on her feet.

"Yes you can. Don't wimp out on me now. It's better if you crouch. In a crouch, you're a smaller target, too. Now get down on your knee. Here. I'll show you first." I got down on one knee. Kept the left up. Put my left elbow on my left knee and pretended to cradle the rifle."

"If you're right-handed do it like that. Your turn."

She went to hand the AK over to me. "Nope. It's all yours, Anya, and it's still your turn."

She almost tipped over. At the last second she steadied and managed to grip the weapon securely.

"Now. See how the mag hangs down like that? You can't lie flat unless you have a support to get behind. With two taped together, it's even worse. That's why the crouch and the one knee up."

"It keeps the rifle supported and the magazines out of the way," she said.

"You got it, girl. Now aim."

I got down on both knees behind her. Reached around. Helped support the rifle. "Pull the butt end in tight to your shoulder. Hold it firm. Now rack the handle. Remember that? What's it going to do?"

"Put a round in the chamber."

"Right. You're my number one mercenary."

She fumbled to find the handle while struggling with the weight of the rifle and the mag. Managed to get it racked. I checked to make sure the slide was on semi-auto.

"Now pull the trigger. One time. Release. Be ready to crap your pants."

The AK barked once. She leaned back against me as I continued to support her grip on the rifle.

"Lean forward. Lean forward. Not back. You have to lean into it. Again. Pull it again. And again."

Six rounds barked. An orange tracer lit up the daylight as it went downrange.

"Did you see that? The tracer round?"

"I did. It didn't go anywhere I was aiming. And holy shit. Does this thing make noise."

"Did you close your eyes?" I asked.

"No. I don't think so? I tried not to. Maybe I did."

"In that case, aim and fire again. By aim, I mean look where you're going to shoot."

She did as I instructed, and a huge grin took over her face when she released the trigger.

"Do you think you could do that without me to support you?"

"I think so. If I had to. I don't want to, though. I'd want you with me."

"Good answer. I'll carry it back to shore. You deal with the ammo bag."

It was hot going. The sun was over our heads. We didn't get the cooling breeze until we got close to shore. We were forced to work our way back to shore through thick brush. She was too far ahead of me.

"Wait, Anya. Wait."

She turned to look back.

"What is it?"

"There are rattlers and scorpions in this part of the peninsula. Don't step on one."

"Son of a bitch. Now you tell me."

"Do you kiss your mother and father with that mouth, woman?" I asked, grinning.

She looked at me, confused at first, before the look turned into a smile. "Well ya. But not often. And my dad doesn't live with us any more."

We were almost at the freshwater stream. My foot slipped. I tripped and stumbled into a water-filled sinkhole. The ground gave way. I was slipping waist-deep into muck-filled water and I wasn't stopping.

"Anya!"

She looked back and screamed. I kicked my feet, using the movement to halt my descent.

EIGHTEEN

It wasn't working. I was into it now. Every movement I attempted. I tried plenty. They only sunk me deeper into the morass of mud and sand. I ceased struggling. It was that, or sink out of sight. I twisted my head frantically from side to side, seeking a branch or roots or anything to pull myself out of my predicament. There was nothing.

Anya scrambled to get to me. She froze when she recognized my predicament. She covered her mouth with both hands to stifle the scream. It didn't do any good. She took two steps back and I started to wonder if she would be any help at all. Wide eyes and hand wringing said panic.

"Anya. Stop. Don't come any closer."

She blubbered. She cried. None of it was what I needed. I tried short and forceful. "Get down. On your stomach. Do it now."

She got down on hands and knees and began making her way toward me.

"Careful. Don't get too close. Take the AK. You know what to do."

"Jim. I can't." She sobbed uncontrollably. Her entire body shook. She was on the edge of losing it completely.

"Yes you can. Take off the ammo bag and remove the strap."

She looked at me. "What?"

All she had to do was listen. Why couldn't she do it? "We're going to need the strap. Take it off. Do it now."

She did, and maybe I praised her a little too much. "I'm going to hand off the rifle. You know what to do. Remember what I showed you."

I made sure I kept the muzzle aimed at me. She reached for the stock. Grabbed it with one hand. It slipped from her grip. "I'm sorry. My hands are sweaty." She wiped them on her pants and tried again.

"It's all right. You're doing good. Now remove the magazine and clear it. Remember?

"I remember," she assured me.

She tipped the mag out, raised the muzzle to the sky, and racked. A shell exited and fell to the ground at her feet.

"Pick that up. We might need it at some point."

"You're pretty bossy for someone sinking out of sight without me."

We laughed. Nervous. Almost uncontrollably. The mood didn't last long. "Okay. Now tie the strap from the AK to the other one. That's it. You're doing good. You've got a nice long rope. You have to find some secure footing. Maybe gather some of those rocks. Twigs. Anything you can find to make a support."

I wasn't sinking any deeper. That was good. I just might make it to the panga yet. Anya collected stones and sticks and made a pile. When she was satisfied, she tossed me the end of the strap.

"Brace yourself. I'm a lot heavier than you."

We reached and stretched. Huffed and puffed. If hard breathing was any measure of progress, we made a lot. But it took forever as I eased myself slowly toward her. I worked both elbows, sinking them into the soft ground. I stretched out flat, like someone who fell through ice.

It worked.

I kicked and strained and pulled and Anya slipped and braced herself and slipped again. My feet popped out of the sinkhole with shoes intact. Anya collapsed, huffing and puffing and out of breath. I went down beside her. I was in the same shape.

"You're hired."

We took a break and caught our breath. I secured the strap to the AK. Anya's shaking hands fastened the strap to the ammo bag. I rolled onto my back and stared at the sky. She did the same. I needed to lighten the mood, more for her benefit than mine. "It sure is a nice day."

"It is, isn't it?"

It was more than a few minutes before we were calm enough to make our way to shore.

"That calls for a beer. You want one? I'm going for a swim."

She popped the top on the bottle and took a long, cool drink, mimicking my own. "Something tells me that's not the first beer you've tasted."

She grinned. "I'd say you were right." She tipped the bottle in my direction. "But it just might be the best one so far."

When I returned the beer was done. She headed off to

take her turn in the pond and came back clean and refreshed.

"Anya?"

"Yes?"

"I'm glad you're here. I wouldn't have made it without you."

"I was scared the whole time, Jimmy."

I couldn't lie to her. "So was I."

NINETEEN

We **took our** time once we were back at the campsite. We moved slowly, almost trance-like. Perhaps we were almost too relieved we were safe. Our guard was down as we rejoiced at the good fortune that shone down on us. I motioned for Anya to be still. When she refused to shut up I covered her mouth with a hand and pulled her to me.

"There's someone out there." I uncovered her mouth.

"What is it?"

I held up a hand, cautioning her to be quiet. I listened between the waves washing ashore, intent on hearing the sound again. "We should get going." I lowered my voice and bent to put my lips to her ear.

"Not yet. Can you hear it?" Maybe her younger ears were better than mine.

"Sounds like a dune buggy."

Except it didn't. The engine sound I thought I heard disappeared into the wind.

"Yes. Voices," she said. "It's probably more picnickers. Like us, Jim."

"Yeah, no. And we're not on a picnic, remember? Did

you notice when we were out in the desert? There are no roads or towns around here. This is buggy country."

A dune buggy's fat tires could traverse the sand beach in a hurry, floating above it. I heard them again. Voices. Growing louder. Men. Talking. Excited. Maybe they were onto us. Maybe they wanted a panga. Maybe they wanted Anya. She stood up and draped the AK's strap over her shoulder. It hung low and pointed straight ahead. Her hand moved to cover the grip. My handgun was still on the panga. A lot of good it would do us there.

"Grip it with both hands. If you fire it holding it that way, the muzzle will kick the wrong way and you'll miss."

She nodded and did it immediately. She didn't bother taking time to look at me.

"That's my girl. Now let's see what they want." I called out. "Hola, hermanos."

The chatter halted. Teenagers by the look of it. Older teenagers. One of them moved to place his hand behind his back. I knew right away what he wanted.

"I wouldn't, cabrón. She knows how to use it."

Did she remember? Would she remember? I had to be sure. I moved behind Anya. I wanted to work myself into a position to take over the AK if she froze. Actually, that wasn't it entirely. I knew she'd freeze. I needed to be there for both of us.

"Chula, your gabacho is hiding behind your skirt. Kiss him goodbye and come with me. I will take care of you."

I moved closer to her. Anya didn't avert her eyes. Didn't bother to look. She knew. Instead, she laughed.

Loud and plain. Racked the AK. Kept on laughing. Cabrón number one's smile faded. Three pairs of astonished eyes widened, not believing what they just witnessed.

"I don't think so, pistolero. Drop the gun on the ground. It's where it belongs when you're with this chula."

Holy shit. Could she play a part or what? But I'd have to spank her later. We had our hands full right now. Or rather, Anya did. She made sure to move the muzzle in a slow arc. Halted when it pointed at the loudmouth. "Are you deaf?" Her hand tightened on the rifle's grip. Cabrón's hand started to move again.

It was my turn to talk. "Slowly. Grip it with your fingers. Only your fingers."

"Do what the gabacho says. If you pull it out any other way, you're dead." Anya's voice quavered.

Was I the only one to notice? It was time to go. "Do as she says and live, cabrón. Do as she says. Are the rest of you armed?"

Hands went up. Heads shook. That made me happy. If I could believe them.

"Then drop it and walk away. All of you. If you come back—"

Cabrón relaxed his grip on the handgun and it landed on the sand with a wet slap. Three pairs of feet beat a retreat so fast they almost kicked up a dust cloud in the wet sand

"That was quick. You did good. Girl, you are a bad-ass. Where did you learn your Spanish?"

Anya's knees gave out. I reached for her. Caught her before she went down. I allowed her to slip through my arms to her knees in the sand. She shook and shivered all the way. "Quick? Dude. It feels like it should be tomorrow already."

The dune buggy fired up and made sounds like it was racing toward a finish line.

"No sweat, chula. Tomorrow we'll be partying it up in Cabo. Tonight we're having a camp-out."

"Promises. Why can't we keep going now? It's not that far by the GPS."

I slipped the AK from her shoulder and turned it toward her and that's when I noticed.

"What? What's wrong? I did good, didn't I?" Anya asked.

"You sure did. But it's a good thing you didn't have to pull the trigger."

Her eyes traveled from me to the AK. Her jaw dropped. She sank back onto the sand. Her eyes found mine. "Holy shit."

"Holy shit is right. You didn't have a magazine."

TWENTY

It **wasn't so** far to Cabo. But once I got us there, I needed a full day to do what I had to do. Number one on my list was getting Anya on an airplane to home. I didn't tell her that, of course, but she had to know it. Didn't she?

"Have you got warm clothes in that bag of yours?"

"A windbreaker and a sweater," she said.

"You need to change into long pants. And socks. I'm going out to the panga to get my bag. In the meantime, gather all the driftwood you can. The bigger, the better. Be sure you take the AK with you. On your back is okay. They won't be coming back tonight."

"Then why do I need to take the AK?" She crossed her arms and frowned.

"I could be wrong," I warned her.

"Thanks for that. I think."

Still, she looked worried. I couldn't blame her. I wasn't being a great confidence builder beyond telling her how great she was when push came to shove. I changed the subject.

"There's a tarp tucked away on the panga. I'll get

that, too. It's going to be cold tonight with the wind off the Pacific."

I stripped to my underwear and waded to the panga. By the time I was back, I was covered in goosebumps and shivering like a dog shaking itself after a bath. In my absence Anya managed to gather a small pile of driftwood. I dressed before helping her gather more wood, and the exercise warmed me some. The big pieces were heavy, and we ended up huffing and puffing as we dragged them to our firepit.

"Help me dig a depression in the sand. I'll collect rocks when we're done."

Anya was a great helper. Maybe she'd been a guide in a past life, but I didn't ask. It was none of my business. Besides, I didn't want her to think she was becoming any more of a necessary evil to tag along only when I needed her for backup. I had to get her on that damned plane.

"Is there any phone service out here?"

"I don't know. My phone is dead."

So much for making a reservation. She'd have to do it tomorrow. Surely she had a credit card. How else would did she get down to La Paz? But all that didn't matter now. The sun began to slowly turn orange as it dipped into the Pacific. It was time to light the fire and begin telling tales from the dark side.

"I'm going to collect more driftwood before it gets completely dark. We'll need more. You stay by the fire and nurse it, okay?"

I slung the AK and took off. I wanted a quick look-see for the three cabrones before the fading light turned into black night. I tracked them as far as I could in the beach sand. Eventually the trail went cold when it was washed away by the surf. Satisfied, I returned with an armload of wood to a roaring fire.

And no Anya.

I called her name. Cupped my hands to my mouth and yelled. Screamed as loud as I could into the wind. Hoped she could hear me. A single set of footprints wandered off toward the bush. Maybe she was taking another swim. I chased after them. She straightened and appeared out of nowhere surrounded by the greenery around the pond.

"I had to pee. What's the fuss about?"

"Next time you have to go, tell me about it, okay?"

"So now you're some pee pervert or what?"

"Anya—"

"Fine."

I knew from experience. When that word crossed her lips I wouldn't be getting anything else out of her.

We finished off the sandwiches and the beer. I told ghost stories and we laughed and she told better ones and we laughed harder. Eventually, full stomachs, a long day and a blazing hot fire took its toll. I made her put her jacket on before wrapping the tarp around her.

"You'll freeze out there, Jim."

She opened it up but I declined. It wasn't big enough for two anyway.

TWENTY-ONE

Last night's warm driftwood fire was down to ashes. Beside me, Anya shivered in her sleep. I eased out from beneath the tarp, trying not to disturb the girl. I adjusted her jacket and tucked the tarp around her still sleeping form.

I jabbed a stick into the remnants of the fire in a feeble attempt to revive the embers. There was nothing. I tossed what was left of the driftwood on, hoping it might catch. I took another swipe with the stick. Outside of building a new fire, we would have to endure the cold. Waiting would delay the inevitable.

The sun was coming up, evidenced by the purple light of dawn. A thin sliver of an orange ball peeked over the eastern horizon. It wasn't enough to shine down and warm us. It was going to be a cold morning, thanks to the wind still coming off the Pacific.

It was time to go. "Daylight in the swamp. Rise and shine, chula." A groan issued from beneath the tarp. "It's alive. She's alive."

Anya peeked out. Groaned and shuddered. Yanked the stiff tarp closed. Called out from beneath it. "I have to pee."

"Is that a complaint? I'm afraid I can't help you in that department."

"Well, you did ask me to inform you the next time. It's the next time."

I tried a little reverse psychology. "Fine."

She half-smiled and crawled out from beneath the tarp to wander off. She crashed through the bushes in her search for a suitable spot. After a long pause, splashing sounds from the pond and loud cursing told me she was suitably chastised. The cold water face-washing had its desired effect and she returned, pink-faced, refreshed, and freezing.

"I'll do the same and we'll be on our way."

It wasn't a stretch to convince Anya to let me carry her to the panga. I stripped down to my underwear and got busy. She insisted on carrying the ammo bag. She would have taken the AK too, but I wouldn't let her. I made the boat and struggled to lift her over the gunnel. She almost slipped from my arms. I tightened my grip and heaved.

"Are you trying to guess my weight, or are you going to put me aboard?"

She should have clued in that I was huffing and puffing and trying to do just that. "Smartypants. I have to be kind to you or you'll take off without me, won't you?"

She laughed and fired up the engines in preparation for our getaway.

"Can I take you into shore a bit? It looks like the tide is in."

I raised anchor and she eased the panga's bow forward. "Not too much throttle. If we go aground we'll both be freezing in the water."

I eased back into the cold water and floated the cooler with her backpack on top. She reached over for her bag and I hoisted the now empty cooler.

"Why are we bringing that? It's empty."

"We'll fill it for the return. And it's not ours to leave behind."

"Jim—"

She pointed down the shore. Last night's interlopers were riding the dune buggy toward our campsite. I inserted a mag into the AK and shouldered it. I got off a quick burst. Brass clinked on the bottom of the fastboat. Sand kicked up and the buggy halted. The driver made a wide turn and the trio retreated in a hurry.

"We're almost ready to go."

The engines were warm. Anya was bundled in her jacket and long pants. I broke out the tarp as a half-assed windbreak for both of us. We'd be able to huddle behind it. Even so, it would be cold and miserable until we hit the harbor at Cabo.

"Hand over your phone."

"It's dead."

"I know. Give me the cable. I have a plan."

I flipped up the dash cover and plugged it in. The charge light came on. I flipped through her search pages and my name popped up in two of them. I showed her the results. "Did you learn anything?"

"I did. You're a private detective. Your business is

successful. You have a reputation for honesty and most of your clients are happy with your results. You don't do divorce work. Also, whoever designed your web page did a fantastic job."

Andrea. She was murdered in my office by a jealous boyfriend.

"Yeah, well, for her trouble she ended up dead. Killed by an acquaintance of hers. Did you notice the mural in the interior shot of the office?"

"I did. It's amazing. And I'm sorry to hear that."

"Andrea did it before she was killed. We kept it as a reminder of how amazing she was in real life. She was such a wonderful person."

I felt responsible for her murder, but I didn't let on to Anya. Why was I telling her this? She didn't need to know. She probably didn't even care. I couldn't shut up, though.

"I hired her part-time. Took her away from her job as a bartender. She was paying off her college bills and jumped at the chance to work two jobs to do it."

I pretty much ran out of steam at that point. I changed the subject. "How far to Cabo? Does that fancy GPS system tell you that?"

Anya ignored me. "Did she end up a partner in the detective business? She sounds pretty good at what she did."

"No. My business partner is Maddie. She's my romantic partner, too."

Yeah. Maddie. She was going to skin me alive when I showed up. Throughout my confession Anya was fiddling with the GPS on the boat.

"Did you get us a distance to Cabo?"

I rambled on long enough. I needed to stop crying in my beer.

"It looks like about an hour and forty-five. No more than two anyway. I hope it's warmer there."

I tucked the AK away in a compartment. One thing about a go-fast panga drug boat. There were plenty of places to stash things.

When we rounded Cabo Falso and cruised past El Arco, I was comfortable enough to get out of my warm clothes. At some point Anya must have slipped into a bathing suit and some filmy number. She made her way past me to the front of the panga. She stood erect with arms out. Her robe trailed behind her. I eased the throttles back, worried she might fly away, like a bird, never to be seen again.

We were only too happy to greet the warm air with smiles and sunscreen. I throttled back a second time and took us into port. An excited Anya finally relaxed and took in the sights. Her head swiveled from the cruise ships to take in several of the many yachts anchored in the protected bay.

"Wow. They're huge when you get to see them from our tiny little boat." She waved and grinned and a couple of sightseers waved back from the heights. "I feel like a millionaire."

Little did she know she was sharing a boat with a half-millionaire who had cash stashed in three Cabo banks.

"In that case, wait until we get closer to our mooring. You won't feel so wealthy when you get a look at some of the yachts tied up beside us."

Cabo. Finally. I sighed inwardly and felt I could relax. Now my problem was retrieving suitcases stuffed with cash from three banks. I had to get them safely to the panga before someone took it from me. I'd been around this part of the world long enough to know that word travels fast when large amounts of cash are involved.

And that wasn't all. I still had a teenager I needed to put on an airplane.

"Call your folks and tell them you're on your way home as soon as you can get on a flight."

Anya frowned and looked disappointed. "Do I have to?"

"Yes. You have to. I'm going to see to it personally. And no backtalk."

"Fine."

There was that word again. I was back to babysitting.

TWENTY-TWO

I throttled back to just above idle and steered the panga slowly through the packed marina. Empty berths appeared to be at a premium, especially for a boat arriving unannounced. I considered calling ahead to book one. Since César's demise, I wanted to keep on the down-low as best I could. The marauding SUVs pulling out of his road were still on my mind.

I had plenty of time to think about what happened to César on the drive to La Paz. Someone he dealt with regarding the arrangements for the armor plating, or the firearms, or the panga, must have put two and two together. Were the Baja buggy cabrones on the beach part of it? Were it not for Anya's presence, I might have taken prisoners and asked some questions. As it was, I didn't want to put her in danger. Letting them go was a mistake, perhaps, but worrying about it now was a waste of time.

I idled our fastboat past huge, expensive yachts populated by millionaires and their suntanned blonde mistresses. Some looked us over with disdain. Anya didn't seem to mind. She stared back, wide-eyed with disbelief at the wanton display of wealth. Hell, she was more attractive than most of the women. Younger, too, which they wouldn't like in the slightest. My face flushed, and I turned my attention back to finding a berth.

Another giant yacht loomed over the panga. As we drifted past, Anya pointed from the bow. An empty berth on the other side was just wide enough for us. I slowed even more and positioned the panga to reverse into it. It was too late. One after the other the panga's three engines stumbled and quit. We were out of fuel.

"Grab a paddle, sailor. We need to row into our berth."

"So now I'm downgraded to sailor? I thought you promoted me to captain of this sinking ship."

"You can take it up with HR later," I grinned at her. "Help me get us into that berth and I'll think about restoring your rank."

Reluctantly Anya turned away from the bow and made her way back to the cockpit. I located paddles in a compartment and had them waiting. She grabbed one and we struggled to maneuver into the waiting berth. It was a heavy, ungainly boat, unwieldy in length for a couple of lightweight oarsmen such as us. A crewman from the neighboring yacht called out from the wharf and I threw him a line. I wasn't fooled. He was checking out my shipmate.

All eyes were on Anya, twisting and pulling on the paddle. It kept her too busy to notice curious eyes and the jealous women checking out her young, lithe body. When they recognized her for what she was, the eyes turned toward me with renewed interest. My face grew hot and I studiously avoided returning the looks. Anya wasn't fooled.

"They're checking you out after seeing me."

So she was paying attention after all. Even teenage women didn't miss a beat. "Yeah, well, they probably think you're my daughter." I knew that wouldn't cut it, and I regretted saying it instantly. "Or something."

She definitely wasn't fooled. I changed the subject real fast, but not before my face turned beet-red. "Hand me those ropes. I need to tie down the boat."

She did as she was told and I tied us off.

"I need your phone."

She handed it over without complaint. My mind raced, trying to figure how to get cash from the banks to the boat all by myself. There was enough bulk to require three suitcases. And transport. A taxi wouldn't do.

And then there was Anya. I needed to book a flight and get her to the airport. And when that was done, I needed to get home. As fast as I could. Maddie was going to kill me. I knew that already. I was about to punch in the office number and then thought better of it. In for a penny, in for a half a million dollars. Wasn't that how the expression went?

The stalled panga drifted against the berth. A loud bang announced our arrival as it bumped the wharf. My lack of recent sailing experience was showing. I handed back the phone and Anya tucked it into the front of her bikini.

"Lower the bumpers. Both sides," I told her.

"Bumpers? What bumpers? Where are they?"

"Those round white and blue things you've been parked on since we got into harbor."

She moved from bow to stern, flipping them over the side. She looked pleased with herself.

"Don't forget the other side, sailor."

I whistled and a wharf rat ran toward us sporting a toothy grin and a name embroidered on his shirt. Reynaldo knew by the silent docking we'd be taking on a lot of fuel. He knew by the look of the panga that it was a go-fast. He knew too there would be plenty of tips in the works if he treated us right.

"Be sure to check all the tanks, por favor."

What did I know? Maybe there was more than two. Barring unforeseen problems on the way north, we'd still need every gallon that could be crammed into the tanks to get to the river bed south of Todos.

Reynaldo nodded and went back to watching Anya pull on shorts and a t-shirt over the bikini. I needed to talk to her about changing in front of strangers. She didn't seem to mind, though. I guessed she thought the wharf rat was good-looking in a teenage kind of way. Just what I needed. A guy sniffing around when all I wanted was to wheel the money aboard and take off as quick as I could.

And one more thing—I needed to get Anya out of the way and onto an airplane.

"I need your phone for real this time."

"Does it have to be right now? I was going to insta some of the pictures I took."

"Insta? What's that?"

Anya rolled her eyes. "That site. Surely you heard of it. Where everyone posts their vacation pics. All the cool people—"

I didn't give her a chance to go on. "Anya." I hesitated.

"What?" She was going into fine mode again, minus the bent knee and the tapping foot.

"I need you to listen to me. Promise you will."

She sat on the gunnel and waited impatiently for an old man to start talking. Her eyes wandered from yacht to yacht, checking them out, before settling on me again.

"You can't post anything about this trip until I get home. If you get there ahead of me, you can't post anything. Understand? Nothing. Nada. Comprende?"

I watched her carefully, looking for a sign that she understood the magnitude of the problem. Should I explain it all to her? Or hope for the best?

"All right. I'll do that."

"I'm serious, Anya. Remember the cabrones on the beach? I don't know if they were after me. Maybe they were looking for someone like you. You need to remember that before you do that insta thing you mentioned, okay?"

"I said okay, Jimmy." She gave me another exasperated okay, and that was the end of it.

"All right. Now give me your phone."

She wasn't so sure about handing it over. "You're not going to delete all my pics, are you?"

TWENTY-THREE

I turned away from Anya. There was no sense letting her know my business. I located a wrinkled piece of paper in my wallet and unfolded it. An old number. Faded. Difficult to make out. I kept it all these years. It was from another life. A happier life. Until it wasn't so happy any more.

I hesitated. Did I want to involve anyone else in my scheme? I considered what I would need, instead. A spare body. A vehicle. A place to spend a night that was off the grid. That wouldn't be the real problem, though. The rest of it would.

There was no one else I knew down here—except for Anya. I already knew she wouldn't be any help. Hell, she was a teenager. The best I could hope from her would be a distraction for the wharf rat.

I hit send and waited. After more than a few rings from the Unknown number that would be showing up, a questioning Hola? said I needed to talk fast. I cast a glance in Anya's direction. She was all ears.

"Who are you calling, Jimmy? Do you know anyone down here? Are you calling home? Maddie must be worried about you by now."

Shit. I forgot I mentioned my partner, Maddie, to the girl. Now what do I do? I hung up, embarrassed at being caught out. I tucked the phone in my pocket while an impatient Anya walked down the pier, intent on surveying the yachts.

I was certain she was looking for trouble, but it gave me time to make my call without her listening over my shoulder. With the call concluded, I settled in for a wait in the hot sun. Reynaldo was busy fueling the panga. Anya halted to chat with him. I was about to give up when screeching tires invaded the parking lot.

I turned to investigate. A car pulled up to the gate. The door swung open and a good-looking, dark-skinned Mexican woman got out and waved frantically. She called my name and I waved and grinned in recognition.

My former wife's sister. Dulce. She took one look and grinned back like I hadn't seen a woman do in a long time. Anya noticed right away. I couldn't tell if that was bad or good. Her hands were on her hips and she was tapping a foot on the wharf, so it probably wasn't good. As if that wasn't enough, for good measure she had a knee splayed out at a sharp angle. I called out to the woman as she ran down the wharf toward me.

"Dulce. It's good to see you."

Dulce didn't waste time wrapping her arms around me. I was forced to pick her up or she would have slipped to the wharf. Out of the corner of my eye I caught Anya giving the poor woman stink-eye. Or maybe it was me getting the stink-eye. More of something I didn't need—a jealous teenager. What did she have to be jealous of?

"Jeem. It's been a long time. I am so sorry."

Dulce and I were intent on catching up when I heard Anya coughing behind me. Right. How could I forget about the girl?

"Dulce. I want you to meet Anya. She helped get me here in one piece. I'll tell you all about it later, okay?"

The two women looked to be sizing each other up. It didn't seem to me like it was going swimmingly. Neither of them was any slouch in the looks department. I'd just spent two days in close quarters with Anya and picnicked on a beach with the woman. I was damned if I could figure out why she was so annoyed with me. Hadn't I just got her within a taxi ride of an airport and a plane ride home? It was what I promised I'd do, after all.

As for Dulce, well, she was my deceased wife's younger sister. There was nothing beyond that. Well, that, and she was beautiful. Hell, they were both beautiful if I thought about it. I tried not to think about it.

"I need to get Anya on a plane home. I'm going to need some help with transporting some things to the boat after that."

I didn't say anything about half a million dollars. What was the point in tempting fate? Maybe if I didn't say anything, she'd think it was drugs. Why else would I have a go-fast tied up in a Cabo marina?

Dulce took a quick glance in Anya's direction and smiled. She appeared pleased the girl would be out of the way in a matter of hours. The question concerning what it was, exactly, that needed loading onto a go-fast panga was never asked.

"I can take her to the airport while you're looking after your business. How does that sound?"

It sounded good, except. Except I needed transport from the banks to the dock. Except I needed suitcases. I needed someone I could trust. Judging by the look on Anya's face, it wasn't so good for her, either.

"I'd like to do some shopping while I'm here," Anya said. "I know I'll never be back."

Dulce was only too happy to hear that. "I can help you with that, too. Whenever you are ready."

I was happy. Anya would soon be someone else's problem.

"While you two are busy, I'll put the boat to bed. I'll see you back here in a couple of hours."

Anya didn't appear happy when I gazed at Dulce and not at her. I didn't care. The sun was out. The sky was blue. I was warming nicely in the sunshine after the boat run across the cold Pacific.

Anya retrieved her backpack from the panga. In her haste to desert me, she whispered something almost unintelligible. Except. I heard every word. They cut like a knife.

"Jeem? Is she serious? She speaks better English than both of us. There's something not right about her, Jeem."

Anya's sarcasm made the warning difficult to ignore.

"Watch out. She'll take you for a ride, and I don't mean in her car or a panga."

I sputtered and she turned to Dulce, ignoring me. "I

need to get cleaned up."

"Come with me, Anya.

The girl threw her backpack over her shoulder and together the women walked to Dulce's car.

TWENTY-FOUR

Maybe **I was** being overly cautious, but I didn't think so, considering what I was after. It was the last of the cash from a freelance job I did years ago. A reward of sorts I split with a former partner. So yeah, I needed to be cautious. The cartels were moving into the resort towns to reap the profits from the drugs they sold to all comers. Any neutrality in these places was out the window.

So here I was. In the middle of it. I might say I was happy to be here. And I was. As long as I got my cash and got out. Get in. Do the job. Get out. Just like old times. Except it was new times. With new problems.

Problem number one was Anya. Except she was headed to the airport, thanks to Dulce. My deceased wife's sister. My wife, Pilar, killed in a plane crash and branded a terrorist. Up to now I had that all in the past, but seeing her sister again—

I shut it out. Tried to. I had things to do. And problem one was solved by Dulce, who volunteered to transport Anya to the airport. That was easy.

While Dulce made for the car, she got busy making arrangements for a flight. Anya returned to board the panga. "I forgot something," she said.

It rocked gently from side to side as she stepped on board. Sure. Why not? I forgot things too. She scrambled to collect whatever it was. Out of the corner of my eye I caught her slipping the handgun into her bag. The one we took on the beach. That wasn't good. An understatement if there ever was one.

"Anya—"

She ignored me and slipped something else into her bag. I didn't care, whatever it was. The gun was key. I stepped onto the panga. The boat rocked with my weight and water slapped again.

"You can't take the gun with you. They won't let you on the airplane. And they'll lock you up. It's not even registered if you declare it."

Trying to reason with a teenager wasn't my thing, especially when she had a loaded handgun. I was about ready to put her over my knee.

"I already checked the action. It's empty. The magazine is full."

Well, at least she got that right. Hell, what was I thinking? I couldn't let her take the automatic with her, even if we had rescued it and it couldn't be traced back to us.

Anya regarded Dulce. The woman's back was turned and she halted partway down the wharf. She was talking hurriedly in Spanish. I had no idea what she was saying, but I figured it was something to do with the airport.

"I don't trust her, Jimmy. How did she get here so fast? She's trouble. I can tell."

Right. A teenager with second sight. The woman thought she was a clairvoyant. Next she'd be asking for a Ouija board. I turned my back to Dulce and eased toward Anya. I didn't want Dulce to see me making a grab for the handgun.

"If you take it I'll make a scene. The locals won't like finding out you kidnapped me for a sex party."

Crap. I had no one to blame but myself. I looked helplessly in Dulce's direction. She was still busy with her phone. "It's your funeral at the airport. I won't be there to save your ass."

"And who saved whose ass on the beach? Your captain, if I remember correctly."

There was no sense denying it. The woman hauled me out of a mud pit. Dulce chose that instant to hang up."

"All right, Jeem. I arranged a flight for Anya. We can go now."

Anya's smug expression told me to shut up, so I shut up. She wouldn't be my problem any longer. "Can we go shopping first, Dulce? You can help me pick out some clothes. I need to clean up before getting on the plane, too."

With women bonding over shopping, what could a man do? I nodded and smiled. With babysitting duties successfully handed off, I was just happy to be here all over again.

TWENTY-FIVE

I needed a burn phone. I took a last look at the panga moored to the dock. Reynaldo was back to take care of the fueling after he went off to do a more prosperous yacht owner's bidding. He knew his job. And his customers. I slipped him some cash and asked him to keep an eye on the panga, por favor.

Reynaldo nodded and grinned and pocketed the cash with nary a look around before getting busy. I turned to walk away before remembering.

"Por favor, comprar un teléfono." My fractured Spanish appeared to work. Compared to most of the gabachos tied up on the wharf, I was probably one of a very few who made an attempt to converse in his native tongue.

Reynaldo gave up his fueling duties and escorted me to the end of the dock, where he gesticulated while giving me broken English directions. I thanked him profusely and slipped him another ten. Paying up front meant he'd probably tell his friends about el turista gabacho when he went off shift. I didn't have a problem with that. It wouldn't be long before I'd be needing all the people I could get on my side.

I shouldered my backpack and made for the store. It was early, but the streets were starting to fill with hung-over gabachos in search of the first drink of the day. Wives dragged husbands to stalls that opened early, searching for last bargains before catching a ship or a plane.

Not to be outdone, I stopped often to check out the storefront merchandise. I strode across narrow streets and meandered through flea market stalls. I was checking for a tail. The markets provided good cover, allowing me to stop and check my six as often as I wanted.

It was the long way to the phone store, but I was okay with it. I wasn't rushed for time. I took my time perusing the display until I found what I wanted. The owner did his best to convince me I needed the latest model with Bluetooth and a high-res display. I dug out my cash and he was forced to settle for the flip phone I needed.

It might not be the most modern tech, but I couldn't be tracked beyond a network tower when the phone was turned on. Like the salesman, Anya wouldn't be impressed with my choice, either. And then I remembered I was rid of her, thanks to Dulce. It wouldn't matter what the girl thought.

I had everything I needed. I put in Dulce's number from my wallet, and flipped the phone closed. A charge wouldn't hurt, but I could probably do that at a café if I stopped for a cold drink.

Next on my list was checking out the location of the banks. It was more than a few years since I'd been in this part of the world. I thanked my lucky stars for that while fighting the tourist rush. I still needed to look casual while doing it. I continued my meandering until I located banco number one.

It wasn't so distant from where the panga was moored. Going by memory, the others were a lot farther apart. Again from memory, I figured I'd need three suitcases. That wasn't the problem, though. The problem would be attempting to tow three suitcases through the streets of Cabo as they filled with cash. I didn't have enough hands, even if I was stupid enough to try. Damn. Maybe I had unceremoniously dumped Anya too soon. But then I had Dulce.

And Dulce had a car. Problems two and three solved. It was turning into a piece of cake after all.

I hit send and this time Dulce answered the phone a lot quicker.

"Jeem?" She sounded awfully happy to hear my voice. I harked back to Anya's warning. And ignored it. Dulce was my sister-in-law. I could trust her.

"Si. Did you get Anya to the airport?"

I wanted to ask if she watched the girl get on the plane. But then thought, why would she not? Anya was going home. Then I remembered the handgun tucked into her backpack. Would she be crazy enough to try to board an airplane like that? The headstrong teenager was no longer my problem. Relief flooded over me.

"Oh yes. I took her to a few tourist stores like she wanted. I helped her pick out a bathing suit and some shorts and skirts. She seemed very happy.

Women. Throw in some shopping and they're good

to go. As soon as the thought crossed my mind, Maddie intruded. She'd kick my rear if she heard me say something like that.

"Good. I'm glad to be rid of her. I was getting tired of babysitting."

"You don't have anyone to babysit anyone now. What are your plans, Jeem? Do you have a place to stay?"

TWENTY-SIX

Bad luck had me arriving in Cabo on a Sunday. The banks I needed were closed until Monday. That left me with an afternoon to kill. And an evening and overnight. I knew a good hotel up on Zaragoza. It wasn't far, no more than a quick walk from downtown. Out of the way. A pool to cool off. A small café. It would be perfect.

And then Dulce made the offer. How could I turn her down? It would make me appear unfriendly, and I didn't want that. I could get caught up on my sister-in-law's family. After all, I made sure Pilar's life insurance went to her grandmother and her sisters, to take care of them. It was a lot of money that meant they'd be sitting pretty for a long time.

The decision wasn't difficult. I asked Dulce to meet me at the wharf in a couple of hours. I needed time to do some mapping to organize my bank withdrawals.

I walked the Paseo de la Marina around the harbor and ended up at an Oxxo where I picked up a paper map. I needed to make sure I had the bank locations clear in my mind. I also wanted to make sure I could use the harbor in a pinch to make good my escape with suitcases stuffed with cash.

Was I worried about it? Of course. I had to transport bags of money to my panga and get out as fast as I could. Even if I had to leave like a dog in the night, I wanted out in a hurry. It might not be possible if I didn't at least reconnoiter the harbor for escape routes. Even if there was only one way in and one way out. Cruise ships and yachts too big for docking would provide limited cover.

Satisfied, I retraced my steps on the Paseo to the marina and made for the banks. I pretended to be a gabacho turista all over again. I walked the routes I would need to take, looking for anything that would get in my way.

I retraced my steps, this time looking for cover. Tourists would provide a lot of it. If the crap hit the fan, there would be a chance they would become collateral damage. I didn't want that, but—

I'd take my chances. I marked the routes on the map and took another look at the situation. Without a doubt, I'd encounter problems, even if it was only jammed sidewalks slowing me down. There was no way around that.

Suitcases. I needed at least two. I considered duffel bags, but that would be too obvious. Bags full of something, presumably cash or drugs or both, might be too common for a lot of people in Cabo. Cartel spies in particular. Common suitcases, on the other hand, were a dime a dozen with the tourists.

I stopped at a store and picked up a waterproof jacket with a hood and another pair of long pants. I stashed them in my backpack and remembered the go-fast keys. I checked my pockets. Nothing. I went through the pockets on the backpack. Still nothing.

I paid and rushed out of the store to land on a bench. Panicked, I dumped the contents of my backpack on the seat. I rummaged through the mess of wrinkled clothes and the detritus I'd collected with shaking hands. Nothing. Where the hell—

Anya. The woman's furtive movements on board the panga before Dulce hauled her off to shop. The little—

I didn't finish the thought. I dumped everything back into my bag and double-timed it to the panga. When I got to the wharf I broke into a run.

I stepped aboard. The fastboat rocked from side to side. Water slapped. My eyes roamed the cockpit deck. I got down on hands and knees and crawled into corners. I pressed seat cushions and ran my hands along the spaces between them. My fingers came up empty. Nada. I leaned over a gunnel and looked down into water too dark and deep to make anything out.

I jumped onto the wharf. There was nothing to see there, either. I chased down Reynaldo and asked, but he only shook his head. Suspicion confirmed.

Anya had the keys. Who else? The wharf rat? I didn't think I'd left him alone before happily waving goodbye to Anya. Dulce hadn't gotten anywhere near the boat. To add insult to injury, Anya had been the one to hijack the pistol, too.

No wonder she was happy to leave. She knew I wouldn't be going anywhere without her. Did that mean she was still in Cabo? She wouldn't have been allowed on the plane with a firearm. Either she was in jail, or—

She was still in Cabo. I flipped open the burn phone, intending to call Anya. I couldn't do it. I didn't have her number.

TWENTY-SEVEN

I cursed my incompetence and got up from my hands and knees to look into dark brown eyes framed by long black hair. The woman's breathing was labored. "Is everything all right?" I looked past Dulce toward shore.

"No, no, Jeem. Everything is good. I took Anya to my place so she could clean up and then we went shopping. Like she wanted. I just came from the airport."

It was a relief to hear. "Good. I was getting tired of babysitting the girl. She needs to get home."

I went back to studying Dulce. Just a bit of eye makeup to emphasize them and a bit of lip gloss completed the look. She'd changed into a slinky, filmy skirt and a matching blouse. The almost sheer blouse revealed she wasn't wearing a bra, not that I had a complaint. She carried the look off too well, and she knew it when she caught me checking her out. I blushed.

"Te gusta, Jeem?"

I was caught. How could I say no?"

"Si. Me gusta."

"Bueno. Estoy contento." Dulce twirled. Her skirt flared, revealing just enough to make me wonder. "Let's go to the car, Jeem."

She took my arm and I felt a warm, firm breast press gently against me before she withdrew it. The sensation reappeared, and then was gone again. Unintentional or not, the woman was working her magic. To what purpose, I wondered. Then she withdrew her arm from mine, and we strolled side by side to the car.

"I'm taking you to my place. I have something for you."

"I opened the door and she got in. Her skirt slipped, revealing well-shaped legs. It was her turn to blush. By the time I got in, she'd strategically adjusted her skirt to reveal just enough that she caught me looking again.

"Te gusto mucho, Jeem." Dulce looked across at me and smiled. "Voy a estar en el problema? Am I in trouble?"

She started the car and hesitated before putting it in gear. Our eyes met and we blushed. I didn't answer her. Maybe we were both in trouble.

"Creo que te gusta mirarme."

I liked looking, that's for sure.

Did I trust Dulce? Did I have any reason not to might be a better question. I didn't really know the woman. Of course, she was Pilar's sister. I'd spent no time with her family beyond getting ready for the wedding. Once married, bride and groom left family behind. Pilar and I high-tailed it to the resort where I was working. It was Pilar who regularly traveled back and forth to visit with family in Tijuana. I was always working.

Perhaps even better, I had no reason not to trust her. "I'm here to pick up something I have stashed in a bank."

There it was, out in the open. She'd be putting two and two together, I was pretty sure. I didn't give her the chance. She continued steering around Cabo's mangled, noisy traffic. I had to explain. "It's cash. A lot of it. And I'm going to need your help."

Dulce looked across at me and smiled. "Of course. Whatever you need. You were good and kind to us after Pilar died. I'm sure I can find a way to repay you."

If good and kind meant sending them every penny of Pilar's life insurance I had coming, then yes. I was good and kind. She leaned on the horn and cursed every time traffic came to a halt.

"All I need is a car and a driver. I'll do the rest."

She looked across at me again. Her face had taken on a serious look. "You won't be robbing any banks, will you? That boat you have, that panga. It is used for smuggling. Are you smuggling drugs, Jeem?"

There it was again. A tiny corner of my brain told me her English was better than that. So had Anya. In fact, I knew it was. She'd been speaking it perfectly since we met up on the wharf.

"No, I'm not smuggling drugs. I'm down here to retrieve what is rightfully mine. I'll be taking it home with me. Nothing more complicated than that."

A plainly visible look of relief crossed her face. She believed me. "Bueno. I couldn't be a party to anything like that."

The traffic started moving again and a dune buggy

pulled up beside us on the busy street. It stayed that way, roaring exhaust drowning out any conversation. Dulce looked out and shook her head. A deafening roar accompanied the buggy as it sped off, leaving a cloud of exhaust in its wake as it weaved through traffic.

"What is it? What's wrong?" Why was she shaking her head?

"What? Nada. Nada is wrong, Jeem. I was just thinking how peaceful it would be if all those things ran out of gas."

Dune buggies weren't unusual in Cabo. Hell, gabacho tourists rented them all the time. This one looked vaguely familiar, I had to admit. The three cabrones from the beach came immediately to mind.

"Do you know them?" I asked.

She twisted her head in my direction so fast her hair followed and cascaded down her front. "Of course not. No. How would I know them?"

Was she being too defensive? I didn't have time to assess. She steered down a side street without slowing and stopped in front of a newer three-story apartment building. "Here we are. Mi casa."

I got out and waited for her to walk around. She took my arm, and there was that breast again. It was getting difficult to ignore.

"We'll drop your things off and you can get cleaned up. I must go to the supermercado if you're going to stay for dinner."

How could I say no? I hadn't had genuine Mexican cooking for longer than I cared to remember.

Dulce's apartment was roomy enough that she had furnished it well. A smaller wall was adorned with pictures of her family. Me with Pilar when we were married at her abuelita's in Tijuana. Expressionist paintings populated several more walls. I finished with my inspection and turned to her. "You have an eye for art."

She waved a hand dismissively. "Oh, I see something I like and I buy it. Nothing is expensive. I try different things. You know."

I was reminded of Pilar. Dulce was just like her sister.

"Here. Follow me."

I grabbed my bag and she led me down the narrow hallway.

"Put your things in the bedroom. The bathroom is across the hall."

She turned and brushed against me before walking out and closing the door behind her. I stripped off my shirt and crossed the hall to the shower. I pretended not to notice her eyes on me from the living room. I cleaned up and changed my shirt and I was ready to go.

Except.

Except Dulce was being too friendly. She didn't really know anything about me now, or ever. Sure, I married her sister. But it was more than a few years ago. From then to now had to be a blank for her. As was she for me.

Maybe I needed my head examined, but I was going to ask Dulce to help me collect the money. Once I had it in the bag, I'd make for the panga and blow this place for good.

She didn't need to know that, of course.

"We can walk to the supermercado, no? It is not so far," she said.

The day turned hot and muggy by the time we ventured out into the street to the grocery store. The Cabo sun beat down with nary a hint of a breeze to soften the heat. Dulce's blouse began sticking in all the right places. She pulled it out and fanned herself, but that didn't work for long. After a few minutes, it was freshly glued to her body, emphasizing her breasts in no small measure.

"I should have put on something else I think." She blushed a bright pink, and by then we were at the market.

"I'm not looking." But I was. She knew it.

"I think you are just saying that."

We both laughed. Dulce headed for the coolers. She opened a door and fanned herself. Whether on purpose or not, the cool air did its thing, and she didn't waste time looking to see if I was watching the performance. "That is better. Now let us shop."

She took me from aisle to aisle, always staying ahead. I enjoyed the view, in no small measure. She pointed and I threw items in the basket. We passed a small selection of flowers and I picked out a bouquet.

"For me? You shouldn't, Jeem."

She didn't refuse when I placed them in the basket anyway. We were giggling like a couple of teenagers by the time we made it to the checkout. A smile of recognition greeted Dulce as she approached the woman at the till.

Something about a nuevo mano or some such passed between the two. I waited and paid the bill and Dulce blushed and rushed me out of the store.

"What was that about?"

She took my arm and leaned in. "Oh nothing. She thinks I have a new boyfriend." She looked up at me with huge brown eyes and changed the subject. "Do you like Mexican cooking?"

"Are you kidding? Pilar spoiled me with it every day," I told her. "I am so looking forward to being spoiled by you."

"You will have to help. That is my fee," she said.

"So I have to pay?"

"Of course. You will pay."

TWENTY-EIGHT

A **car roared** past. Noisy exhaust drowned out our conversation. I flinched reflexively, recalling the Baja buggy on the beach. Dulce's reaction to the dune buggy passing her car on the busy street came immediately to mind. Dulce stumbled and fell against me. The bag of groceries slipped from my hand. I caught her and surrounded her in my arms. She leaned against me and collapsed. I tightened my arms.

"Are you all right?"

She stayed with me. Her own arms wrapped around me as she pulled me close. "My ankle. It hurts." She gripped my forearm and tested her ankle by putting weight on it. At the same time she leaned heavily against me. We were almost at her place.

"Here. Let me get your bag. You can lean on me, all right?"

I circled her waist with my arm. She did the same and we walked together, hips bumping as she limped along. The closer we got to her place, the more she leaned into me. By the time we were at the bottom of the stairs, I was looking up, wondering if she was going to make me carry her. I shouldn't have wondered.

"What is it, Jeem?"

I stifled the grin, remembering Anya's comment about trying to guess her weight when I hoisted her over the panga's gunnel. I had trouble with Anya, too.

"I'm going to have to carry you."

I bent to pick her up. Dulce's arms snaked around my neck. She was lighter than Anya. Shorter, too. Even so, it wasn't going to be easy for this out of shape gringo. By the top step my pink face and constant huffing gave me away. "I'm out of shape for this," I admitted.

"Nonsense. You are just right. Put me down and I'll let you in.

An arm went around me for support as she used her key. I pushed the door open and together we walked in. Dulce's limp appeared to have healed appreciably as she took the grocery bags and placed them on the counter.

"Go and sit in the living room. I will bring you some limonada."

I did as I was told and observed her as she happily performed her host duties with nary a limp. I pretended not to notice when she brought the lemonade.

"I'm going to change." She pulled at her blouse to fan herself. "It is too hot. I am going to take a shower. You can too if you want."

I had a strong sense that she was inviting me to share the shower. I declined as gracefully as I could. "I'll wash the vegetables and set the table while I wait."

It was my feeble attempt to ignore what was going on between us, but it wasn't working. I was being led down a garden path I was only too willing to take. Instead of doing my guest duties, I went and sat on the sofa.

I was about to settle in when Dulce's phone buzzed on the coffee table, distracting me. I reached to check it, scrolling through multiple screens of calls. I had no idea what I was looking for. I gave it up and put the phone back on the table.

The water stopped running and a suitably dry and wet-haired Dulce wearing a robe ventured into the kitchen. After a quick look she returned to sit next to me.

"You changed your mind."

I did. Guilty as charged. Dulce settled in against me with her head on my shoulder. "You don't want to eat right away, Jeem?"

No. I didn't want to eat right away.

Instead, I wanted to feel guilty for how easy it was for Dulce to seduce me. I didn't think of anything else. Not what I was doing down in Mexico. Not my money. Not even Maddie. All of that was the last thing on my mind.

There was one thing, though. Or maybe it was two.

Every time her head moved, the sun streaming through the window reflected a rainbow of light from one or the other diamond stud earrings. I was no diamond expert, but it sure looked to me like they were real.

The rose gold and diamond watch on her wrist didn't appear to be a cheap Rolex knockoff, either. It looked like the real thing. She noticed me looking and moved to pull her arm away.

"What time is it?"

I took her hand in mine and brought it closer. I was

trying to cover for my curiosity. Dulce yawned. Her head came off my shoulder and she straightened up. "It's still early. We have plenty of time, Jeem."

Maybe. Maybe not. But I knew about such things. In the not too distant past I bought a watch just like it for Maddie. It too was no cheap knockoff.

TWENTY-NINE

Dulce stood up and took my hand. Heavy-lidded eyes looked down at me. A sultry smile took over her face. She pulled me up and led me down the hall to the bedroom. She shrugged and the robe slipped from her shoulders, cascading onto the floor. She sat on the bed and reached for my hands. I didn't object. I couldn't. I was too far gone and she knew it.

I ended up surrendering as she pulled me down onto the bed beside her. It was too easy. I didn't have it in me to refuse. I settled in against her, eager to feast my eyes on her naked form in the subdued light. She allowed me to look for the longest time. Finally I had enough of looking and my hands traced the outline of her firm, eager body.

Sweaty sheets stuck to us as we separated and came together again. Eventually we separated and slipped apart, too exhausted to care about how or why or when or if it was over. I collapsed beside her.

We kicked off sheets and tossed wayward pillows off the bed onto the floor. It was quick, and when I finished she slipped next to me. Her body followed my form and curved against mine. An errant arm and a leg ended up on top of me. It was almost too hot to bear.

"You are a good lover, Jeem. Your woman is lucky."

Thoughts of Maddie came flooding back to me. Guilty as charged. I didn't care. I reached for Dulce and pulled her even closer. We were still exploring our bodies in that way new lovers do. I found it to be exhausting work, and eventually I dozed off.

I woke to feel Dulce slipping out of bed. Naked and shameless, she made for the door and disappeared down the hall. She was on the phone. Her muffled voice filtered back to the bedroom. Even with both ears paying attention, my Spanish wasn't good enough. I couldn't make out what she was saying. She finished her call and stood in the doorway, still naked. Smiling. Sated. As was I.

"We need a shower. Come. We can do that together, too." She held out a hand and I took it like I knew what I was doing. But I didn't. I was merely allowing Dulce to lead, and I was willingly following along, blind to everything but her naked body.

I was blind to what she was doing, too. She wasn't giving me time to reflect on what just happened.

THIRTY

My eyes and the rest of me followed Dulce down the hall to her bedroom. She shrugged and the robe slipped from her shoulders to cascade down her body. It fell in the rest of the way to the floor. She halted at the entrance to her bedroom and turned. She leaned back against the entrance, arched her back, and aimed dark-tipped breasts in my direction.

"Come back to bed, Jeem. It is too early. It is more comfortable to wait in here."

No doubt it would be. I hesitated long enough for her to turn and walk into her bedroom. She left the door wide open. A dim light illuminated the outline of her naked, inviting body as she eased onto the bed and waited.

"In case you change your mind."

I changed my mind. She welcomed me into her room yet again. Outstretched arms reached. I eased onto the bed and onto her warm, inviting body. The alluring scent I inhaled earlier greeted me anew.

"Let me take care of you, mi amor."

The pounding wouldn't stop. I forced my eyes open, half awake, groggy with sleep. It was still night. I looked for a clock. Couldn't see one. The banging went on. Dulce lay beside me, unaware of the commotion.

Barely awake, I sat up and swung my feet to the floor. I looked around at the unfamiliar surroundings and changed my mind. It wasn't my door they were beating on. I shook Dulce. She curled into me. Her lips caressed an ear and she murmured.

"Not again. Jeem. You are too much for me."

I shook her again.

"All right. I need a shower first."

She heard the knocking, groaned, and sat up. Her feet found the floor and she sighed as she climbed out of bed. She donned her robe before admonishing me. "Stay here. Be quiet. I will be right back."

She closed the door, leaving me to wonder. Boyfriend? Husband? It was too late to ask. I made a pile with the pillows and leaned back to listen for the door to unlock. Voices filtered into the bedroom past the closed door. High pitched. Too low to hear. Another woman. A hushed conversation. Probably a girlfriend. Something about staying or going or disappearing. Some shuffling and then silence.

Dulce returned. Opened the door only wide enough to allow her to slip through into the bedroom. Whatever it was, it was settled without argument or loud voices. I considered it a victory and pulled the sheet up. I wanted to ask, but it wasn't my business.

The robe slipped from Dulce's shoulders and she hesitated, allowing her body to bathe in the faint light coming through the window. It was for my benefit and I watched, still intrigued. She eased into bed without a word. Her cool body snuggled against my own beneath the sheet. Warm breath on my neck and lips moving against my ear convinced me she wasn't going to take that shower just yet.

THIRTY-ONE

I **checked Dulce's** breathing. She was fast asleep. I hesitated and listened again before easing out of bed. I waited, motionless, before pulling on my pants. I left the bedroom and eased the door closed. The latch clicked and I listened again. Satisfied Dulce was still sleeping, I made my way to the small kitchen.

I wanted coffee. No, I needed coffee. But that wasn't it, either. I needed to do something to pull myself out of the swirling pool of self-loathing and disgust I was sinking into.

Coffee wouldn't do it, but I was desperate to try anything. I ran water and filled the tank and waited for the water to burble and boil. I opened cupboards and found a mug and waited for it to fill before making for the balcony. I slid the door open. Cool night air wafted into the room. It was a welcome relief from the damp, sticky air and willing woman I deserted.

I sipped the hot coffee and listened. There it was again. A rustling sound coming from the living room. I stuck my head around the corner and looked in. Boyfriend? Not likely. At least, I hoped not likely. I hadn't overheard a man's voice. Probably a friend.

Someone who had been out partying and needed a place to sleep. Oh Jeem."

"(A voice I recognized. Mimicking what she overheard. I was too angry to blush. I was at her before I remembered where I was. That the hell are you doing here? Why aren't ne?"

ble I went through to get Anya to Cabo and bound for home was all for nothing. Even nsuccessful. I didn't believe my ears. She had again.

h Jeem."

She sat up, clutched at the sheet to make sure it covered her, and snaked a hand into her backpack. The missing panga keys appeared. She raised her arm and rattled them just to aggravate me even more.

"If I was your father I'd put you over my knee—" I started before she interrupted.

"If you were my father I wouldn't be here." She shook the keys again, grinning the entire time. "You were looking for the keys in the wrong place. I had them all this time. Did you find out how much she weighs yet?"

That was it. We broke out laughing. I shushed her. "Be quiet if you know what's good for you. You want a coffee?" What the hell else could I say? "Anya—" I began.

"I thought you might need them, so I brought them back," she said. "Throw me out if you must, but I'm on your side. And that woman isn't."

"Anya—" She didn't give me a chance to fi

"And by the way, if there's any doubt in yo
by now, I still don't trust her. She's too need
what's with the Oh Jeem I overheard? Doesn't so
that young and good-looking have a boyfriend?"

Anya threw the covers off and got up from the
she was sleeping on. She was in yet another bikini, o
didn't recognize. How many did she own?

"Yes I recognized your voice. You really rocked he
world, didn't you?"

Finally I was allowed to get a word in. "Anya. What
are you doing here? You're supposed to be on a plane
home to safety. Why aren't you on it?"

"I leave with who I came with. I'll be leaving with
you."

"You're going to be trouble for the boys, aren't you?
The color suits you, by the way."

"Thanks. I picked it out myself. I told you when I
left. I wanted to do some shopping. So Dulce took me
shopping. I picked up this suit and some tees and that's
when I saw her talking to one of our cabrones from the
beach."

I didn't believe her. Why would I? I was convinced
she'd say or do anything to avoid going home. She
picked up on that and pulled out her phone.

"It's true. I took a pic. Look." She held out the
phone.

So it was true. It was the cabrón driving the dune
buggy that pulled up along-side of us yesterday. Why

didn't I recognize him then? I realized I was too into Dulce to notice anything.

"What the hell—"

"Yeah, oh Jeem. What the hell. You owe me beeg time. How are we going to dig you out of this bit of quicksand?"

"Very funny, sailor."

"Well, it would be, if I knew what it was that was going on with you. You still haven't told me why you're down here."

I sighed, still reluctant to put her in the loop. Now that she climbed back on board in more ways than one, how could I not trust her? "Money. Cartel money. Half a mil in cash, since you're wondering."

She looked at me incredulously. "Whaaat? How? When? Where? How did you—"

"It's a long story. I'm going back to bed."

"I bet you are. Do I need earplugs?"

"Not yet. Bring your sheet."

I led her out to the balcony and slid the door shut behind us. Anya reached for my mug and took a sip. "Ugh. At least put a bit of sugar in it to make it palatable. Maybe even some chemical."

"Chemical?"

"You know. Sweetener. French vanilla, at least. Get with the program, Jeemie." She grinned up at me and handed back the mug.

"Will you stop calling me that?"

Anya returned to the sofa bed and I sat on the recliner beside her and looked over the bright lights of

Cabo and the harbor. She adjusted the sheet to cover her legs.

"What am I going to tell Dulce? I need her car. And I need to pick up suitcases. Three, to be exact. The cash is in three banks. Then I have to get the suitcases to the panga. And we have to get aboard and leave before that woman leads a cartel sicario to us for the reward."

"A reward? She gets a reward for screwing you?"

"Yeah, no. She'd get half a million bucks for making us think it was the cartel getting the money. After what you told me about seeing our cabrones from the beach, I'm convinced she wants it all for herself."

"She wants something all for herself, that's for sure. And right now, it's all about you."

I blushed and Anya went on. Maybe she didn't notice in the dim light. "She's dangerous, Jim. You know that, right? And she lied to you. To us."

I patted Anya's leg. "I know now. Thanks to you. I'm going back to bed to think."

"So that's what you're calling it now?" She grinned at me. "You lucky dog."

"I might have been before you showed up. Now I know better. Good night. Sleep—"

She grinned right back. "Tight?"

"Smartass."

"You know it, sailor. Your captain has you pegged, even if she's only eighteen."

"Oh shit. I forgot all about it. Happy Birthday, sunshine."

"Yeah, yeah. Don't hug me with those arms until

after you shower."

I turned crimson in a hurry. "You're wise beyond your years, Anya."

"Yeah, thanks to you. Now get back in there and make us proud."

I trudged down the hall, only half wanting to go back to Dulce. Anya's voice followed me down the hall.

"Good night, Jeemie."

The other half wanted to run out the door and down the street, screaming at my stupidity when it came to women. Instead, I made sure to close the bedroom door.

THIRTY-TWO

I lowered myself into bed, not wanting to disturb Dulce. I had a lot to consider and I didn't want a repeat of what went on between us earlier. I eased the covers over her naked and warm, inviting body. She stirred and shifted toward me. A leg and an arm embraced me in her sleep as she nestled beneath the sheet. She murmured something I couldn't make out.

I hid my disappointment from Anya on hearing her tale about seeing our dune buggy cabrón. That wasn't the worst of it. That she'd seen Dulce with him was the problem. I kicked myself for not noticing, but by then I was too into the seductive Dulce. Thanks to Anya, I knew the woman's intentions and mine weren't in sync.

I had no reason to think Anya would make it up after she tamed our cabrones on the beach with the AK. All three of the men would be memorable after that little episode had burned itself into her brain. The picture she showed me sealed it. Now the question became whether I could even use Dulce to help retrieve the cash.

I needed to come up with a plan to get Anya back to the relative safety of the panga in one piece. With my bags of cash. I was back to babysitting again. Would it never end with that girl?

It was all about the car. Dulce's car. How could I keep the woman entertained? How could I keep her thinking she'd be the one to end up with the cash she so desperately wanted? And how the hell did she find out? I never mentioned it to a soul.

Anya. Was she the one giving away the goods? But I never told her about the cash, either. Perhaps she assumed it was drugs. Cash or drugs. Dulce probably didn't care what it was, only that it would end up as easy cash in her hands.

Would Dulce learn I knew what she was up to? Should I even believe Anya? By now it was obvious the girl had her own agenda. That was made more than evident when she didn't board the plane.

Dulce's warm body shifted away from me beneath the sheet. She withdrew her arm and her leg and I eased up and out of bed. I pulled on my pants for a second time and went into the living room. Anya was already up and waiting.

"What did you come up with?" Her voice was low. Almost a whisper.

I cautioned her anyway. "Not too loud. I don't want to wake the woman."

"Judging by her appreciation of your performance I don't think she'll be awake any time soon, Jeem." A toothy grin took over the girl's face as she mimicked Dulce's pronunciation.

"You're quite enjoying this, aren't you, woman?"

"Yes. No. I don't know. We need to come up with a plan. The sooner the better, Jim."

My proper name crossed her lips. Finally. Perhaps now she was taking things more seriously. I pretended I didn't notice. "That's what I was thinking about before I came out here. We need her car. We don't need her."

"But the banks don't open until—" She showed me the map on her phone. I pointed out the banks I needed.

"They don't open until, until—" She tapped at the screen and scrolled frantically. "Darn it, Jim. We've got a different opening time for every one of your banks. Even if we wanted to get an early start, we can't."

"Mexico time," I told her.

"What? What do you mean?" She looked at me quizically.

"It's an expression. No matter what you want to do, no matter how much you plan, it will take a lot longer than you anticipated. Mexico time."

I was faced with a dilemma. If I waited—. No, if we waited in the apartment, Dulce would be up soon. She'd be the one offering up her services, much as she had last night. Except, this time it would be her car she was offering. There would be no way I could refuse and have her not know what she was up to with the cabrones from the beach.

And what about Anya? I was responsible for her now. I couldn't leave her on her own. And if Dulce knew she was the one responsible for my learning about her involvement in the scheme to relieve me of my cash, well, who knows what would happen to the girl. The cartels weren't known for much sympathy when their cash was involved.

"Flip a coin, Anya. Do we involve Dulce, or do we go it alone."

She didn't hesitate. "She's def not on our side. Isn't it better if we keep her close? That way—"

She made sense. "As good as done."

I opened the refrigerator and looked inside. It was well-stocked, thanks to yesterday's trip to the supermercado. "What would you like for breakfast?"

"Pancakes with chocolate chip happy faces, please."

"No sweat. It'll be ready in a jiff."

I found the bacon and a pan and I was good to go. Grease splattered as I whisked eggs and added a little cream. I put a four-sleeve toaster to work with some bread. Anya got busy setting the table with plates. Cutlery clattered and found the correct places for knives and forks. Her mother's doing, probably.

"There's juice in the fridge, too."

She found it and orange juice splashed into empty glasses.

"Will you watch things for me? I'm going to wake up sleeping beauty."

She put her hands on her hips and bent a knee. A foot tapped the floor. By now it was a familiar position. I'd seen her assume it more than a few times.

"With your willpower where she's concerned I better switch everything off and turn up the music."

"Ha-ha."

But she wasn't far wrong. I walked down the hall and turned to look. Anya was shaking her head. I hesitated at the door to the bedroom. I didn't need to wake Dulce up. She was already getting dressed. She turned to face me and finished buttoning her blouse. She still wasn't wearing a bra.

"Last night was amazing, Jeem."

I was beginning to get annoyed with her Jeem. Now that Anya had confirmed what she was about, I was ready for it. "It was for me, too. Breakfast is ready. I'm going for a shower."

Before I knew it she followed me into the bathroom and I was treated to another display of her naked body. I managed to dance through the shower and get out before I did more damage. If Maddie found out—

But I couldn't be thinking of Maddie now. I needed to be thinking about my cash and the building I wanted to buy and kicking myself for not telling Maddie and and—

Anya called out from the kitchen, and it reminded me I needed to be thinking of her safety, too.

"Breakfast is served. Come and get it or I'm throwing it out."

That was all I needed. I fairly danced into the kitchen and sat down. Dulce followed, frowning as she remembered Anya. Whether Dulce liked it or not, Anya was a part of the equation now.

THIRTY-THREE

I made a feeble attempt at small talk, but it was difficult with Anya there. She bore witness to last night's encounter with Dulce, and I was embarrassed that she heard everything. Anya tried to make light of it earlier, but it still burned bright, and my face flushed at the sudden memory.

"What is it, Jeem? What's wrong?"

A quick frown crossed my face at Dulce's fracturing of my name. I was on to her now, thanks to Anya. Still, I didn't want Dulce to know. Beneath the table, Anya connected with a kick to my shin. I would end up bruised for a week.

"Well—" I hesitated. It was a meaningful pause. Even Anya regarded me. She had to be wondering how much I was going to reveal. "I have a problem, Dulce."

She looked across the table at Anya before reaching for my hand. Her eyes met mine. "I tried to put Anya on the plane yesterday. It's not my fault she wouldn't get on."

Dulce looked back and forth between us. She was doing a good job of demonstrating her lack of sympathy for the girl's predicament.

"What are your plans now, Anya? Have you decided to stay in Cabo for a while instead?"

It sounded like Dulce was washing her hands of the girl, just as I tried to do. We both failed spectacularly.

"Well, I'd like to stay on for a bit." It was Anya's turn to look at me. "I just turned eighteen, so I can drink now. I thought I might hang out and visit a few bars and generally have some good, clean fun. What do you think, Jim?"

She regarded me and smiled sweetly. Teenagers. I didn't know whether I wanted to spank her or hug her.

"It's out of my hands, Anya. I tried to get you on a plane for home and you decided you wanted something else. I'm not responsible for you any longer. You're on your own."

The look of disappointment that crossed Anya's face was palpable. We never discussed this turn of events. Nor had we even considered it. Shit. I had to do something. Anything. I didn't want Anya free to wander around Cabo when I would be in Dulce's car rounding up the cash. Anya would be coming home with me or else.

It was my turn to kick her beneath the table. It was only a light tap, but she almost jumped up out of her chair. Her hands slapped the table and she shifted in the chair. "Maybe I'll tag along with you two for a bit, then. To get the lay of the land. Isn't that what they say?"

"Why not? What do you think, Dulce?"

Not that I cared what Dulce thought. Anya would be with me or else. I'd be leaving with the one I brought.

Now all I needed to know was the day of the week. "It's Monday, right?"

It had to be Monday. There was no way in hell it couldn't be. I turned from one to the other, expecting confirmation. Instead, all I got were confused looks before Anya stabbed at her phone and brought up a calendar. She took her thumb off the thing and Sunday came into view. I raised an eyebrow and regarded her from across the table.

"Well, Anya. You're eighteen now. I'm going to take you drinking. Are you coming, Dulce?"

Shit. I was a day late and a dollar short. My delay at César's to armor plate the van had cost me more time than I counted on. And the lengthy drive south to La Paz took even more given my fatigue. What I'd been hoping would be Thursday or Friday was in fact Sunday. No banks today.

"I have some errands to do, Jeem. Do you still have my number in that relic phone you carry? Call me later, por favor."

I patted my pocket and nodded sheepishly.

"Are you ready, Anya? It's time."

We were barely out the door before Anya started in on me. "Are you crazy, Jimmy? We need to get away from that woman, not encourage her to join us later. She's a crook. She can't be trusted. How many ways do I have to say it before you get it?"

On and on she went. When she finally halted to take a breath, it was my turn.

"We need her car. And we need to check those banks

again. Are you sure they're all closed today?"

I opened the back door of the cab waiting at the entrance to Dulce's apartment and Anya got in. I jumped in beside her. "Why was this waiting? Was it just for us?"

"We'll never know. My Mexican isn't that good any more. Just roll with it and we'll figure it out as we go. Now check those banks again."

She busied herself pulling up the bank web pages. "We're in luck. There's one."

THIRTY-FOUR

The cab dodged cars and pedestrians on its way downtown. Already the tourist action was beginning. The usual gringo suspects roamed the vendors and the stores, wandering aimlessly, moving from one street vendor to another, one store to another. Women with husbands in tow picked things up and set them back down. Heads nodded or shook, while wives tried quick-marching to cash registers before husbands changed their minds.

I allowed Anya to take the lead. She moved as aimlessly as the rest of them, wandering back and forth and up and down the various streets. I was still suspicious about the waiting taxi. I kept an eye on our six for a tail. If there was one, he was good.

Finally Anya turned into another market, and I was relieved. I could take a breather.

"I'll wait for you here, all right?"

She rocked from side to side and wrung her hands. "You won't leave me, will you?" She bit her lip.

My eyes found hers in an attempt to reassure her. I raised a hand to her shoulder. "No, Anya. I won't leave you. If you're not here, I'll wait."

Reassured, she wandered off. I was left to my own devices. I pretended to be something I wasn't—a gringo turista—a gabacho, in Mexican slang. I didn't care. I was more concerned about the taxi cab that was waiting at Dulce's door. I wanted to know if I was being followed. If we were being followed.

I left the market and made for the street. Plenty of plate glass would allow me to keep an eye on my six. I strolled, wandering aimlessly and then pausing, pretending to look into windows. Nothing caught my attention. No one looked back at me. No one turned away. Plenty of dark glasses on just about every tourist in sight. Behind my own dark glasses my eyes wandered from side to side. Searching. Checking.

All clear.

I popped into an expensive-looking store with too much inventory and a lot of bright lights. I chose an overpriced duffel in a size I thought was big enough. I waved away the approaching sales person intent on up-selling and made for the register. I shook the dust off my credit card and paid. I slung the empty bag over my shoulder and I was good to go.

I exited the store and turned left and traveled half a block. I halted suddenly and pretended I forgot something before turning to go in the opposite direction. I passed the store and looked in. Someone was talking to the sales person. The conversation halted when I came into view and I pulled away immediately. My pace quickened as I searched for a distraction.

A rack of sunglasses presented itself. I hid behind it and kept an eye on the storefront. Sure enough, the man walked out. His eyes scanned the street. His lips moved. He had to be cursing for losing sight of me. Or he was talking into a microphone.

I waited him out and he disappeared into the crowded street. I made my way to the only open bank in Cabo on a Sunday.

The staff was friendly and accommodating when I asked to get into my safety deposit box. I showed my passport. My name was checked against a list. I filled out a form and signed it. My signature was checked. People conferred. They must have been satisfied. I was led to the vault.

The bank official unlocked the gate and accompanied me into the vault. We inserted keys. He went to stand by the open vault door, and I wondered if it was protocol to observe patrons as they rifled through their boxes. I hesitated and cleared my throat and he left.

It was time.

I slid the heavy box from the wall and hefted it onto the steel table where I opened it. Cash in good old U.S. dollars. I didn't hesitate for a second. I unzipped the bag, reached into the box, and proceeded to empty it. I finished and closed the box and left it on the table with the key. I had no further use for it.

I hefted the duffel. It was too ungainly to throw

over a shoulder. Besides, that would look suspicious, too much like a cartel mule. Instead, I allowed it to hang from my shoulder. It was much more comfortable that way. I passed the counter and threw a smile and a jaunty wave in their direction before exiting the bank.

I made my way through the crowded street to the market where I left instructions for Anya to wait for me. I casually strolled through, halting occasionally to look over the crowd. It should have been easy to spot her if she was where I told her to wait.

She wasn't.

THIRTY-FIVE

I wasn't happy with Anya. I was stuck holding a bag stuffed with money weighing me down like an albatross. I couldn't find Anya, even though I was pretty sure she was shopping her heart out. I wandered aimlessly, jostled by sweaty tourists for what seemed like forever. The growing heat in the noonday sun didn't help improve my patience.

I passed a bar and a noisy, cheering crowd spilling out onto the sidewalk. Someone counted down on the bar's PA system. I stopped to listen. Positioned to get a better look at what was going on. It was barely noon. The revelers, mostly male, were drunk as skunks. A commotion in a corner of the room drew my attention. I made my way past pillars and dodged tables on my way to the crowded corner. It was standing room only. Someone hung upside-down in a contraption designed to do just that.

I looked closer. It was a woman. The yelling increased. Fists waved. I looked again. It was my woman. Well, okay, not my woman. It was Anya. Hanging upside down. Holy shit. A man beside her held a funnel. Another poured beer into it. Amber liquid drained down a clear plastic tube into Anya's mouth. She coughed and sputtered and swallowed and burped and gagged.

That wasn't the worst of it. Her skirt was over her stomach. Her top would have covered her face had it made it past her chin. Thankfully she was wearing a bikini beneath it all. That, or she owned the most colorful underwear of any woman I knew. Except, she was a teenager. Eighteen, but still.

I made my way through the crowd of picture takers. It probably wouldn't make a difference, but I had to try. "She's underage. You'll go to jail."

A disappointed groan interrupted the chanting. I picked the girl up and unhooked her feet from the contraption. I slung her over my shoulder. She struggled and kicked and almost slipped off. I tightened my grip and walked out of the bar to a crowd of clapping, fist-waving men.

"All right, woman. When I put you down, it's going to be over my knee. You know that, right?"

Her spiel began immediately. "Oh Jeem—"

"Can it, woman. We're going to the boat. I've already been to a bank. We need to stash the cash."

"Wait. Put me down."

She struggled and wriggled and kicked. Nothing landed. Arms flailed, but didn't connect. I trudged onto the dock. The wharf rat took one look before grinning and shaking his head.

"It looks to me like you have your hands full, señor."

I didn't reply. I was busy with a flailing Anya. I leaned

down and dropped her on her feet on the wharf. I didn't give her a chance to move before I picked her up and stepped onto the panga.

"Are you guessing my weight again, Jeem?"

The boat rocked. Water slapped. She rushed to make the gunnel, leaned over the panga's side, and projectile vomited into the water.

"Happy Birthday," I called to her.

She groaned and bent over the side. Splashed water on her face. Tried to straighten and lost her balance. She made a grab for the gunnel and missed. I made a grab for her hair and connected. I pulled her back into the boat. I smacked her ass, hard. She straightened and rubbed at it. I expected a dirty look, but she must have known better.

"What are we doing here? Are we leaving already?" She went on rubbing at her pink rear.

"No. You're throwing up. That's what you're doing here. As for me, I was cashing out at the only bank that was open."

"Oh god. I'm going to be sick again."

She was, too. It was too good to miss. "That'll teach ya. Now get your ass back on that dock and distract—"

Loud applause from the women on the surrounding yachts echoed over the water. Anya took a bow and threw up again. This time, she managed to stay standing.

"When you're done, get your ass up on that dock and distract everyone you can think of while I put the bag away. We have two more to go and the banks don't open until tomorrow.

She groaned. Did as she was told. She stripped off her clothes to display the assets. She bent over and adjusted the bottom and I ducked out of sight, not wanting to be witness to her performance any more than necessary.

Besides, I had cash to stash.

THIRTY-SIX

I didn't give Anya time to be hung over. "Are you ready? We're heading back to Dulce's."

"What, you didn't get your fill last night? By the sound if it, she got hers."

"Do you kiss your mother's cheek with that mouth?" I wondered.

"Not when you're going to be around, that's for sure."

"Don't worry about it, kid. What happens in Cabo, stays in Cabo," I informed her.

"Oh good. I was beginning to worry I'd have to tattle on you if you tattled on me."

I tut-tutted and never-minded and we were off. I flagged a cab and we returned to where we started. I tried the door. It was unlocked. "You might like a shower about now, woman."

Anya trotted down the hall to the bathroom. The water ran and then halted. A hair dryer whined. She exited wrapped in a towel and grabbed her backpack. When she returned, she was suitably attired in shorts and a blouse. "What do you think, Nash?" she asked.

"You look a lot better than the last time I saw your

teenage ass hanging upside-down in some nameless bar. You sound better, too."

She grinned back at me. "Thanks. I think. Now what?"

"I think we should go for a walk. I need to know if there's anyone keeping an eye on us. And whatever you do, do not admit to Dulce I've already been to one bank. I have an idea how we're going to accomplish the other two."

Anya donned her spotless Air Force 1s and I marveled again at the luminescence. How she managed not to vomit on them was beyond me. She danced down the stairs ahead of me. I could tell she was hangover-hurting, but I didn't say a word. If she could pretend, so could I.

"So what's the plan, Stan?"

I turned left and she followed me for half a block before I crossed the street. I reversed course to take us in the direction of downtown. "Let's scout out the remaining banks. I want to plan our escape."

"What about bags? Did you get them yet?"

I gave her a dirty look. "No. The only bag was hanging off my shoulder," I said.

"That's not a nice thing to say to an impressionable teenager. Especially a female."

"No, silly. I meant the bag of cash I had over my other shoulder," I explained.

"Oh. Of course. I should have pick-pocketed you. How remiss of me not to notice."

"That's one way of putting it, I guess." I couldn't keep a straight face to save my life. I broke out laughing and Anya joined in. "You're some piece of work, woman. You'll be giving the boys a run for their money if I know anything about women."

"Yeah, no. If you knew anything about women you wouldn't have ended up in bed with—"

"Can you let it go? I was doing research," I tried telling her.

"Yeah, I heard your research, all right? One damn fine job it was, too."

I halted in the middle of the sidewalk, put my hands on my hips, and tapped a toe. "Fine."
Her grin was bigger than mine, but not by much. "Touché, mister detective. Now tell me your plan to get the remaining two bags on board."

THIRTY-SEVEN

I led Anya to the harbor and along the malecón. I wanted to show her how we'd make our way out to sea from the confines of the berth. "Climb up on the bench with me." I pointed out the cruise ship in the harbor. "If that liner is still anchored, we need to get it between us and shore. If it isn't, and there's another one, we use it."

"To block anyone from seeing us."

Dulce and her cabrones still weighed heavily. Anya had her mind made up. The girl was dead set against having anything to do with Dulce. My thinking was that we should use her if we could.

"Jim?"

"What? Yes. As much as possible. It might work. It might not. We won't know until we try."

"It looks like it's a long way out," she said.

"That's the salt air haze off the ocean making it look distant. It's closer than it looks. You'll see when we get out there tomorrow."

It was a pretty wide-open harbor once we were free of the wharf. Yachts and cruise ships. If anyone was after us, we'd need to make use of whatever was out there. There was always the chance any pursuers would think we might be servicing the yachts.

"Do you think we should refill the cooler today? Lots of ice and some of those burritos? They should keep a couple of days in the cold."

I regarded Anya with fresh eyes. She was thinking. Growing up fast. "How about some beer, too? Sol is good. You'll probably like it."

She groaned and I laughed. "Trust me. You will. Especially in the heat of the moment. Sunglasses. Long pants. Long-sleeved shirt. Cap. Bandana times two for the sun on your neck. Do you have all that, woman? Or do we need another shopping expedition before we head home?"

Home? Why had I just called Dulce's place home?

"Well—"

"Okay." I was resigned. "I guess we're going shopping."

"Perfect. But we're not going home. We're going to our temporary accommodations. And you get to spend another night in that woman's bed."

Anya's voice took on a sour note. I considered what she said, and it was true. If we went back to Dulce's, I'd be back in her bed in a heartbeat. The pattern was established last night. I slowed and led us to an empty bench. "Climb up here with me. You can see better."

Again I pointed out what we needed to do once we got the panga sea-borne. I halted before going on about our accommodations.

"We could make our way to this place I know. It's within walking distance. We can go by Dulce's on the way and pick up our things. Go back to the suitcase store. Pick up the bags and make our way. What do you think?"

Anya didn't answer right away. I could almost hear the wheels turning.

"What if she's there? No way will she let you get away." She hesitated before going on. "I could go back and collect our things. She'll let me leave in a heartbeat and there won't be any fond farewells to deal with. I'll jam your pack into mine and we're good to go."

"After all that shopping?"

"I'll pick up a duffel. She won't know the dif."

Dilemma solved. If only it were that simple. We made our way to the store and picked up a couple of expensive aluminum carry-ons. Anya added a trendy duffel to the mix. I paid cash, and we were good to go.

"How are we going to work this, Anya?" We passed by a coffee shop, and she halted.

"This will be perfect. Wait here." She handed over the carry-on and took the duffel. "I'll be back in a bit. Don't do anything I wouldn't do."

I gave her a toothy grin. "So then, I can kill some time by hanging upside-down and chugging beer from a funnel?"

"Too funny."

I turned and she was gone.

THIRTY-EIGHT

I **threw caution** to the wind and settled into my café con leche manchado in the crowded coffee shop. I was forced to sit with my back to the door. It wasn't a position I liked to be in at the best of times. Down here, waiting to pick up a pile of cash while associating with a woman who might want to take it all away from me, well, forewarned was forearmed in my book. Still, I was feeling pretty good about things. I marveled at how it was all coming together with only a few minor bumps in the road.

"Jeem."

I recognized the familiar voice. My first instinct was to ignore it. I turned in my seat and waved above the mass of people sitting around the tables. At the same time I checked the sight lines into the coffee shop from my seat. If I didn't know better, Dulce had to be following me. She walked up and stood over me, a smile wide on her face.

"Where is your friend?"

Dulce sat down at the small table. A foot brushed my leg. I was certain it was meant as a distraction when her eyes moved to check out the doorway. That's what I should have been doing. The mistake was on me. The slight shake of Dulce's head was suspicious, but when I turned again, there was nothing to see.

"Anya is off shopping," I said. "I had enough walking. We're meeting later."

Like she didn't already know. I wondered if she was spying on us while we walked the malecón.

"I'm on my way to the supermercado to get us something for dinner." She stood to go.

I wanted to say no to dinner, but I was sure it would raise suspicions. Dulce might think I had other ideas—not that I didn't—but she didn't need to know. "All right. We'll see you later, okay?"

My eyes roamed over what was beneath the loose blouse. She noticed my wandering eyes and appeared pleased I was still distracted. I tipped my café in her direction and she was off.

The woman bamboozled me yet again. I regretted accepting the dinner invitation without putting up so much as a maybe. I checked out of the coffee shop behind Dulce and halted to get the lay of the land in a street filled with gringos. If I was being tailed, I was going to have to work to find out. I didn't want to work. I just wanted my money.

I overheard talk of a storm moving in. I checked the sky to the south. A bank of dark, black clouds hung high in the sky. It didn't appear as though they were anything to worry about.

I walked past the bar where I found Anya, wondering if she might have returned to spite me. I didn't hear any yelling or chanting. The hanging tree, as I called it, was unoccupied. I hoped Anya learned her lesson about drink and the devil. I smiled at the remembered Stevenson verse.

"What are you so happy about?"

It was the voice I wanted to hear. I bumped into Anya completely by accident. Bags and boxes filled her arms. She was having a hard time balancing them all.

"What the— Are you taking all that home with you? How am I going to fit on the panga with all of it?"

She grinned and began handing off as much as she could get me to take. I fumbled and mumbled and helped her unload some of it. She fished in her bag and held out the keys to the go-fast, rattling them for effect. "You might not get to come along. With all that cash and all my souvenirs—"

"Yeah, no. I disabled it. You won't be able to start it, girl. Now come with me."

I made a grab her arm and hauled her off toward a shirt shop. This time it was the Harley store. I helped her pick out a nice black tee, long enough to use as a night shirt once she got home. For good measure I threw in a hoodie, too. It would get cold on the Pacific side of the Baja before we made Todos Santos.

"You'll thank me when you get home, trust me. Also, we've been invited for dinner," I informed her.

"Well for crying out loud. Are you going back to that den of iniquity? We could stay on the panga. I'm sure there are more than a few deck hands on those yachts moored in the harbor—"

"Yeah, deck hands that want you on board. Me, not so much. Besides, the devil we know—"

"You mean the devil you know, Jimmy."

I ignored her and tried to look busy hailing a taxi. The driver fought traffic to get us to the dock, where we unloaded and stashed Anya's treasures on board.

"Bring a couple of those bags to Dulce's. We can use them for cover."

Before long we were back in the taxi and on our way to Dulce's. Together we trudged up the stairs. I placed an ear to the door and listened to rattling dishes. I was about to change my mind when Anya banged on the door.

Dulce called out and Anya almost bounded in. The bags toppled to the floor in a pile and I added the one I carried.

"You've been shopping. Good girl. Jeem? What did you get?"

I held out my hands. "Nada." I was more concerned about the two bags I still needed for the remaining banks. And the car. How would I manage to get Dulce's car out from under her?

I went out to the balcony and took a quick look south. The dark clouds looked to be a long way off.

THIRTY-NINE

Dulce's phone rang. She excused herself before answering to take it to the balcony. She eased the door closed and began an animated conversation. She paced back and forth in front of the door. Waved a hand. Looked in at us and smiled. The smile didn't appear genuine. Anya moved to stand out of sight by the door, and then returned to the kitchen, shaking her head.

"She's speaking rapid-fire Spanish. I can't understand a word."

"That's okay," I told Anya." Before she gets back can you check your phone? I overheard some gabachos talking about a storm. The clouds to the south are pretty black and I'm worried about our getaway tomorrow.

Dulce returned from the balcony. She appeared distracted and annoyed and I wondered what her partners in crime had been doing to warrant the scolding they obviously received.

"Where's Anya?" Dulce asked.

I stirred the pot on the stove absentmindedly. "I think she's in the bathroom." I taste-tested the concoction as Dulce sidled up to me. "This is very good. I haven't had anything like this in ages."

She double-barreled her breasts against my arm. It was a movement deliberate and filled with meaning. "I can tell. You made me very happy last night, Jeem."

Dulce blushed and didn't pull away. I tactfully moved out of range just as Anya reappeared. She took one look and rolled her eyes. I frowned and shook my head and wished she wouldn't be so obvious with her disdain for the woman.

Dulce's phone rang again and she made for the balcony. Anya pulled out her phone and used the opportunity to show me the weather map she called up in the bathroom. "You were right. But it's not a storm. It's a hurricane. It's supposed to hit late afternoon."

"Today?" I exclaimed.

"No, no. Tomorrow. We need to make time, Jimmy."

Anya took to calling me that after I admonished her a half-dozen times for using Dulce's pronunciation.

"Can you nab her car keys before we leave?"

"Sure, but what are we going to do about her?" Anya asked.

"Leave that to me," I said.

"There's one more thing, Jimmy. I picked up two bags while you were talking to Dulce in the coffee shop. They're in the trunk of her car. We won't need to go shopping for them tomorrow."

"How did you manage that?"

"There was a suitcase shop right across the street. I was surprised you didn't notice me, actually. Or maybe not. It looked to me like she was purring like a kitten."

I blushed beet red. "Dammit, woman—"

"Don't damn me," she insisted. "You're the sinner here."

I didn't have time for a response before Dulce returned from the balcony, still looking at her phone. "What are you two so deep in conversation about?"

"Anya was wondering how she'd get her stuff to the boat tomorrow morning."

"That is no problemo. I will drive both of you," Dulce insisted.

FORTY

I delayed as long as I could. I insisted on cleaning up and used the dishes as my excuse. Anya caught on and took her sweet time in our conspiracy of two. Maddie would have been proud of me. I blanched, thinking of her and what only just transpired with a conniving Dulce. It had me almost feeling ill.

With the cupboards and drawers back the way we found them, I made a final stab at wiping the counter. I stretched and yawned and mumbled a complaint about eating too much and needing to walk off the effects of the meal.

"I'll come with," Anya said, with a conspiratorial wink.

Dulce wasn't expecting that. She looked at Anya with eyes no bigger than slits and frowned.

"Let's go, Jimmy." Anya made it plain Dulce wasn't invited, but the woman took it graciously enough. I was sure she'd be on the phone the entire time we were away.

Anya called out as we were leaving. "We won't be too long, will we, Jimmy?" She closed the door and we walked to the street. Anya looked up and nudged me. Dulce was on the balcony, backlit by the lights in her apartment. A bent arm said she was on the phone. I didn't need to guess who she was talking to.

"Okay, so the car is loaded with the suitcases you bought, am I right?"

"I already told you that. Or were you too busy checking her out to remember? I know you're weak that way." She giggled.

I couldn't disagree. The street lights weren't bright enough to reveal my embarrassment. "If I didn't think it was perverted I'd put you over my knee—" I began.

"Yeah, yeah, talk is cheap, Jimmy. Who's the pervert again? Now let's talk about tomorrow. We need a plan."

Where had I heard that before? Of course we needed a plan. "So what's your plan, Anya?" That forced her to make with the quiet time. She walked on, thinking, or pretending to. When she halted, I almost bumped into her. I dodged and turned.

"Here's what I see. After you tire her out, you'll tie her up." She rushed to continue, and I didn't get an opportunity to say no. "While you're doing that, I'll get the car keys and load the rest of my stuff. I'll drive you to the banks and park out front. I'll wait for you, and after bank numero dos I'll drive us to the wharf. What do you think?"

It worked for me. In fact, it sounded perfect. We high-fived in agreement.

"Do you want to go back to the scene of the crime right away?" she asked.

"No. Let's be turistas. You want to go back and hang out at that bar where I found you earlier?"

"Very funny, Jimmy. No I do not want to hang out as you so eloquently put it. Where are we going to get food? Despite all that cooking, there's nothing usable we can take away for our boat ride."

"I already stocked the cooler with ice and beer. We'll pick up tacos and burritos on the fly tomorrow. In the meantime, I checked the panga. It's fueled and oiled and good to go, thanks to Reynaldo. Can I have the keys now?

"You won't leave me behind, will you?" she asked, solemnly.

"No, Anya. I plan on leaving with the one I brought." Where had I heard that before?

"Good to know. I felt the same way at the airport when you had Dulce try to ship me out."

"Yeah. About that. I'm sorry. It seemed like the thing to do at the time."

The plan was simple enough. If anything, it was probably too simple. Getting Dulce in bed wouldn't be a problem, though. Tying her up and keeping her there might be. Take the car to the two remaining banks. Load up. Make for the wharf and the panga. Load the boat. Cast off. Todos here we come.

What could go wrong with something so simple?

FORTY-ONE

Anya and I returned to Dulce's in the dim light of the street lamps. We got lucky when someone exited the building. I made a grab for the door. We trudged up the stairs together. Anya halted and whispered at the beginning of the last flight. "The tape is still in my backpack," she said.

"Good. When the bedroom door closes, wait until things get quiet and bring it in."

Anya grabbed my arm and looked at me like I was nuts. "Look, Jimmy. I've done a lot of growing up since I met you, but there's one thing I don't need in my life."

I knew there would be something coming, but I had to ask anyway. "What's that, kiddo?"

"An image of you and Dulce doing the dirty burned into my teenage brain to last until the day I grow senile," she insisted.

"Only next to walking in on your mother and father doing the same thing," I added for good measure and grinned.

"Oh. My. God." She closed her eyes and shuddered. "Do you have to remind me?"

I laughed and bent an ear to Dulce's door.

"What is it?" she asked. "Is there someone in there with her?"

I waved Anya off and knocked on the door. Before Dulce could open it I barged in. Her phone was on speaker and she was listening intently to a male voice. When she saw us she hung up immediately. If there was a guilty look on her face, I couldn't tell.

"Did you have a good walk?" she asked.

"We did. Let's go out on the balcony and enjoy what's left of the evening while we can."

The evening was pleasantly warm. A bit of humidity. A light southerly breeze drifted in across the bay. It was bringing in high overcast from the south, and I remarked on the western horizon turning a bright pink reflecting off the cloud cover. Dulce said something about limonada, and she went inside. The balcony door slid shut behind her.

Anya spoke in a low voice. "Probably more phone calls."

"No doubt. Are we ready?" I was more concerned with Anya's commitment. I already made mine. I needed to know she was ready to do the deed with no regrets—at least, not until we were on board the go-fast and headed north.

"I'm ready. If you need any help hog-tying that woman—say, shouldn't we be drinking our lemonade by now?" Anya asked.

"If you've never had fresh-made limonada, you're going to learn to be patient. It's worth every minute. And what's that about tying up a hog?"

She giggled. "It's only an expression." She got up and went to the door. "Jimmy?"

Now what? Babysitting was getting tiresome when all I really wanted was to sit and relax with a fresh-made lemonade while I enjoyed my last evening in Cabo.

"Jimmy."

Exasperated, I snapped at her. "What? What is it now?"

The sliding door rattled behind me. "I can't get it open. I can't get the door open." A frantic Anya banged on the glass door. "She locked us out."

"Oh for crying out loud." All thoughts of a nice cold drink had flown off the balcony and into the street. I stood up, annoyed and impatient. "Don't tell me you can't open a simple sliding door too. Why do I have to do everything?"

"It's stuck," she said.

I reached past Anya and tried the door. "See? Stuck on the frame. Let me see if I can get it working."

She stood back and I leaned into the task. It's not stuck. It's locked."

Car tires screeched on the street below Dulce's balcony. We bolted to the railing to witness Dulce's car speeding down the street.

"Are you sure it's hers?"

Of course it was. Who else would end up locked out on a balcony on a warm evening in Cabo while waiting for tomorrow to retrieve cash-and-carry from banks that didn't open at the same time of day?

"Dammit Anya—" I halted. It wasn't her fault. It

wasn't anyone's fault. "Yes. It's her car."

It wasn't only her car. I witnessed a Baja buggy pull out and roar off in hot pursuit. I recognized dos cabrones on board. I wondered about the whereabouts of the third man from Anya's AK beach party.

"Two of your three party boys are chasing after Dulce in the buggy, just so you know what's going on."

She rushed back to the railing, but only the sound of the roaring exhaust was left behind. "So I guess now you believe me."

"Fine. If you say so." I couldn't keep a straight face, hard as I tried.

"I'll smack you, Jimmy."

"Nah. We're both having too much fun, don't you think?" I asked.

It might be fun, but we were on dangerous ground. I walked to the railing and looked down. We were too high to do any climbing, up or down. I leaned over as far as I could to the balcony below. I figured I could probably get down to it and try the door. If it was unlocked.

Behind me, the door rattled on its track and bumped against the stop. I straightened and followed Anya through to Dulce's living room. "Hairpin?" I asked.

"What else?"

"You're hired," I told her for the tenth time. "Now what are we going to do to fix this? We need a car."

The quickest way to get one was to use Dulce's. The woman wouldn't be able to follow us without it. Besides, the car's trunk already had everything I needed to collect my cash from the last two banks. Except she was in the wind, and we had no idea if Dulce was coming back.

Do we wait, or do we go?

FORTY-TWO

Anya did a job on the sliding door with a hairpin to unlock it.

"I say we pretend nothing out of the ordinary happened. We were out on the balcony, and now we're in the apartment. No need to mention we had to break in."

"Well, she wanted us locked up for a reason," Anya said.

"She did," I admitted. "And she got away with her compadres, which is what she wanted to do. There's no way she could have taken us with her. We'd have recognized them. It would be obvious what she was up to."

"Yeah, like it isn't already, Jimmy."

I almost asked her to go back to calling me Jeem. "I'm going to make coffee. You want one?"

"How about a beer?"

I checked the fridge. Anya was in luck. A lonely Sol stared back at me. "Hair of the dog."

"Arf."

A comedian, too. The boys were going to love her. She'd give them a run for their money. Which, come to think of it, was exactly what she was doing with me.

"We're going to wait her out. We need the car. Plan A is still on the table."

"What about plan B?" she wanted to know.

I handed off the beer. She twisted the top and flicked it onto the balcony where it bounced once and flew off.

"Plan B? Plan B is see plan A."

"Fine."

We laughed and I had my coffee and Anya had her beer. We were still in deep crap. I hoped she knew it. We returned to the scene of the crime on the balcony and admired the sun setting over the horizon.

"Tomorrow is going to be a big day, Anya. We're deep into enemy territory and Dulce wants all the money. She must think we don't know it. If we can keep her thinking that—"

"That's your job now, Jimmy. It falls on your broad shoulders."

"If you think it's my shoulders that are going to do the grunt work—"

She put her hands on her hips and gave me the look. "You just had to say that, didn't you?"

"You know, Anya, contrary to my seeming enthusiasm for the ways of the flesh, I'm not feeling all that great about being unfaithful."

"So you're feeling just a bit guilty, Jimmy?" she asked.

"Yes I am." I had to admit it. "So remember this—we'll always have Cabo. To quote a friend of mine with some experience in the matter, what happens in Cabo stays in Cabo.

"Thanks. I think. Shit. Here she comes." Anya took

the lead. I was left to internalize my pity party.

"Hi, Dulce. I think we broke your balcony door."

"Is no problemo. I can get it fixed. Where's Jeem?"

"He's here somewhere," Anya said.

The woman halted at the hallway and turned to Anya. "I'm going to bed. Tomorrow is going to be a long day for all of us."

N ot as long as you think it will be, you duplicitous bitch. Together we're going to fix your wagon. Anya said it to herself, but she wanted to scream it out loud.

Jim called for her, interrupting her daydream of vengeance. She rushed down the hall and opened the door. The bedroom was pitch black. "Tell me you're not naked in here."

Anya flicked on the light, revealing Jim bent over Dulce. He was frantically wrapping tape around Dulce's wrists. "I'm not naked in here. Did you want me to be?"

"Too late. Holy shit, Jimmy. You've been busy."

"Do I meet with your approval?"

"You sure do, but I'm not certain Dulce is all that impressed" Anya said.

FORTY-THREE

Dulce struggled against the tape binding her wrists to the chair. I bent to tape her feet. She kicked out and landed a good one on the side of my head. I tried to catch it on her second try and missed. I wouldn't admit defeat. I pulled a black hood out of my pocket and pulled it over her head. "Dammit Anya, help me out here."

"Jimmy?"

"What? What? I'm kinda busy here."

"Do you always walk around with a hood in your pocket?" Anya got down on all fours and scrambled to grab a struggling Dulce's wayward feet. She succeeded with one and I taped it.

"Thanks for the help." I taped the second ankle and sat back to admire my handiwork.

"What's with the hood? Are you— What happened with plan A?"

"This is the new plan, eh?" I grinned.

"You're a regular comedian. What are we going to do with her now?" Anya wanted to know.

I got up off my hands and knees and went to the bedroom window. I opened it and looked down. "It's too far for her to jump. If she manages to get free while we're still here she'll have to come through us." I checked the clock on the nightstand. "It's late. It's past your bedtime. Get out and get to bed."

"Where are you going to sleep?" Anya wanted to know.

"We'll be sharing the sofa. Get used to it."

"No we won't," she insisted.

"Yes we will. I'll take first watch. I'll wake you when it's your turn. Now try to get some sleep."

"Oh. All righty then, Jimmy. In that case I'm going to have a shower. I want to be bright-eyed and bushy-tailed for tomorrow's adventure."

"You read a lot, don't you?"

"How can you tell?" she wanted to know.

It took more than a bit of shoulder shaking to rouse Anya for her watch. That was a good sign. She was getting some well-deserved rest before tomorrow's ordeal. She stretched and I handed off a coffee. "Sorry. There's no more beer in the fridge."

"Probably just as well. I'd be going to the bathroom all night." She threw back the sheet and I closed my eyes.

"You can look. I'm dressed and ready for anything from that bitch."

"Good. Be sure to check on her once in a while," I told her. "I don't want Dulce to choke with her mouth taped."

"You're too good to her, even if she is your sister-in-law."

"I'm not sure how that works with a dead wife. Do you think we're still related?"

Anya shrugged and all I could do was shake my head.

"I'm glad you had that shower." Smirking, I stretched out on the sofa and pulled the sheet over my head and mumbled. "Don't wake me unless it's an emergency."

It wasn't so easy to fall asleep. I tossed and turned and worried and more than once ran through everything I thought could go wrong. The clock on the stove I could see in the kitchen told me that took an hour.

I must have dozed off. A loud bang woke me. The bedroom door. Something was wrong. Still groggy with sleep, I witnessed Anya hurrying down the hall in my direction. She found her backpack and fished inside. Her hand came out with the automatic.

Damn but I'd forgotten all about it. "What are you planning on doing with that?" I wanted to know.

Anya ignored me and ran back down the hall. I scrambled out of bed and ran after her. I arrived too late to witness the destruction in her wake. Dulce's chair lay tipped on its side. Dulce was still taped to it.

"What did you do?"

"Dulce was struggling to breathe," she explained. "I ripped the tape off and she started bad-mouthing me. Then she moved on to you."

"I was sleeping. I didn't mind." I never heard a thing.

"Help me get her up."

Together we lifted Dulce, still taped to the chair. Blood streamed down her face from the cut caused by Anya's pistol-whipping. She tugged the bag back over her head. "How did I do?" she asked.

"Remind me not to cross you, okay?"

"That woman is such a bitch," Anya said.

"Tell me something I don't know, thanks to you. Now hand me that gun before you shoot her, too."

I cleared it and tucked it into the back of my belt. "I'm going back to bed. Nudge me when it's time, dear."

I turned and left before Anya could think of a comeback. It was just as well. Anya was growing up fast and I was proud of her because of it. Kind of like a daughter I never had, I guessed. I called to her as I retreated down the hall.

"You did good, Anya. Keep it up. Put the tape back on her mouth."

FORTY-FOUR

I searched through Anya's backpack, turning pockets inside-out. I tossed what I found on the floor. My fingers closed on them on the bottom of the bag. I pulled the keys out and pocketed them. I found Dulce's car keys on the kitchen counter where she put them when she came in. I stashed them into a pocket for safekeeping before stretching out on the sofa-bed. I must have slipped into slumber almost instantly, because the next thing I knew, I woke to Anya. She was leaning over me and shaking me.

"What is it? What's wrong? What time is it? Did you have to cold-cock that woman again?"

She grinned and handed me a cup of coffee. "No, silly. It's time."

I looked up at her holding the coffee and rubbed the sleep out of my eyes. She was ready for something. "Time for what?"

My eyes moved to the balcony window and the still-closed blackout curtains.

"It's time to go," she said.

"In that case, put the coffee in a go-cup and give me a minute."

I scrambled to find my shoes and rushed down the hall to the bathroom. I splashed water on my face and finger-combed my hair. I scratched at the stubble staring back at me in the mirror.

"Give me another minute to check on our señorita," I called to Anya in the kitchen. I opened the bedroom door. Dulce, awake and in fighting spirit, struggled against her bindings. Blood caked the side of her face where Anya smacked her with the pistol. I didn't feel sorry for the woman. I had better things to do. I ripped off the tape.

"I'll get you some water before we go."

Dulce screamed. Anya ran into the bedroom as I hurried to replace the tape.

"My mistake. I thought she needed a drink. She's a stubborn one, isn't she?"

"Leave her, Jimmy. It's time. Where's the keys?"

"Let's get out of here." I couldn't get us out fast enough. I pushed Anya ahead of me down the hall to the door. I grabbed her arm and pulled her back. "Wait." I put an ear to the door and listened. Nothing. I opened it slowly and looked in both directions. The hall was empty. We were good. "Now we go. I'll lead."

Anya didn't move. She was busy searching through her pack.

"What is it now?"

"Where's the gun? And the panga keys. And the car keys. Where are they, Jimmy? I can't find them!" she exclaimed. Anya's voice was panicky and high-pitched. If she knew what I suspected, it would be even worse.

"It's under control. I have everything. Let's move, dammit."

We descended the stairs. Halted at every level to look out for los cabrones. No one was about. No dune buggy in the street. We tossed everything into the trunk.

"I forgot my shopping." Anya ran off before I could utter word one and suddenly I was the one panicking. I chased her up the stairs three at a time and met her already coming down. "Dammit woman—"

At the car, I tossed her the keys and got in the passenger side. "You're driving."

She turned the key. Nothing happened. "What's wrong now?"

Anya looked down at the shifter on the center console. "Oh. Jimmy? I don't know how to drive stick."

"It's no big deal. Just do what I tell you. Look down," I told her. "See the pedal on the left? That's the clutch. When I tell you, push it in and let it out. In. Out. Just like that."

"Okay. What's the one in the middle for?" She looked down again.

"Never mind that one. See the one on the right?"

"Yes."

"That's the gas."

She rolled her eyes.

"Clutch and gas. That's all there is to it."

"What about this thing?" She patted the gear shift lever.

"I'll work that for you. All you have to do is steer the car and push the clutch in and let it out when I tell you."

"Excellent. When do we start?" she wanted to know.

Roaring exhaust pipes were getting louder.

"Right about now. Push in. That's it. Now turn the key."

The car started and I jammed the shifter into first gear.

"Let it out slow. Good."

The car jerked into the street. The front bobbed up and down. I slammed back and forth against the seat. Anya hung onto the steering wheel with a white-knuckled death grip.

"Push in. Good. Let out. Perfect. Don't forget to look where you're going," I reminded her.

In defiance, Anya looked at me with pursed lips. "Where are we going again?"

"The bank, dear. The bank."

"Oh, right. Sorry."

"In! Push in, dammit."

The engine raced and I yelled and we jerked into gear. I figured we only needed the first three at best. "Good job."

"I'm not your puppy dog, Jimmy."

It was my turn to grin. "You're doing a good job. Who would have known a Florida girl didn't know how to drive stick until now?"

The car began jerking forward. "More gas. Give it more gas. Good. We'll get you a Mexican driver's license yet."

FORTY-FIVE

I called and Anya pushed in the clutch. She was getting better at hitting the gas, too. The car porpoised from first to second. The first bank was coming up fast. I couldn't picture Anya jerking around the block multiple times in first gear while I was inside retrieving my cash from the vault.

"Well look at that. Didn't you get lucky."

She turned into a double space in front of the first bank like a pro. I didn't even have to tell her to hit the brake. I stared through the banco's glass doors. I didn't recognize anything inside. That's how long it had been. A bank is a bank everywhere. An employee appeared to unlock the doors from the inside, and my reverie disappeared in an instant.

It was opening time. I was happy as a drunk finding an open bar first thing in the morning.

"Do you have a rabbit's foot in your bag or what? I won't be long." I hoped. Mexico time might play into it. And why not? Mexico time played into everything else we did down here. "Wait right here. Do not move. No matter what. Understood?"

Anya nodded and looked pleased with herself.

"Yes, you did good, girl. Puppy dog or not." I got out of the car without giving her a chance to wisecrack a response. I scanned the street before making a move. It looked all clear. Whatever that meant. I leaned in through the open passenger window. "Pop the trunk," I told her.

"Pop it yourself." She took the key out of the ignition and shook it. "There's no trunk button in this jalopy."

I retrieved the suitcase and tossed her the key. "Keep it running, Bonnie. We might need a quick getaway."

I made for the bank with bag in hand. Even this early in the morning gringo turistas milled about. Hung over. Half asleep. Sunburned from too much exposure in a hurry. Lethargic after last night's boozing.

I zig-zagged past almost immovable objects intent on buying more souvenirs or looking for more of the dog that bit them. It was obvious by the smell. Many were still wearing yesterday's wrinkled clothes. I shook my head in feigned disgust and carried on into the bank.

A wall of cool air assaulted me full-on. I pushed my sunglasses onto my forehead and proceeded in the direction of what I figured was the vault. A dapper-looking hombre in a suit approached to head me off. I explained what I needed and he led me to a desk in a far corner of the brightly-lit enterprise occupied by a flunky.

I made my request and flashed my passport for identification. In return I got an oily smile. He reached into a drawer and slid a form across the desk. I proceeded to fill out the requisite paperwork. No biggie. It was the second time, and the paper was the same. Only the name of the bank was different.

Flunky checked the form and looked up at me. "Por favor, señor Nash. Follow me."

He nodded to the guard, and I followed him into the vault. He took a key from a ring and inserted it into my box before turning it. I did the same and the door unlocked. I thanked him and he left me alone in the room. I hoisted my overnighter onto the table, opened it, and dumped the contents of the box.

I didn't stop to count.

Banco numero dos was done. Mission accomplished. I exited the vault. On my way out I nodded at the official and tossed the key in his direction. He waved acknowledgment and missed the catch. He was busy on the phone. Maybe he thought I might be another messenger with cash to carry and didn't want to ruffle feathers. That was fine with me, but the phone in his hand said something else.

I didn't wait around to find out. I rushed through the door and made for Anya out front. I knocked on the glass, startling her out of her reverie. "Let's roll."

"Who's Bonnie?" she wanted to know.

"Bonnie Parker. Clyde Barrow. You know."

"Huh?"

"Do a search for them." I was on a high with the cash safely in the back seat.

"Your education on the last century's popular culture is sadly lacking, woman. We'll have to do something about that eventually."

"Yeah, no, I'm a roaring twenties kind of girl, thank

you very much. This century, in case you're wondering."

I couldn't dispute that. I didn't have time. A familiar face rounded a corner. He stopped suddenly and did a double take when he recognized the car. He reached behind, going for a gun. What else would it be?

"Get down! Get down! It's one of your amigos."

It didn't occur to me to draw my own weapon. There were enough tourists on the sidewalk to fill a cruise ship. I jumped from the car and double-timed it toward the cabrón. The handgun wasn't clear of his hip, but he was trying his damnedest. I caught him mid-stride as he leveled the gun in my direction. He fired. The banco's glass shattered into a million pieces and covered the sidewalk.

My football tackle wasn't the greatest, but it did the job. I connected with his knees. It brought him down. I fell on top and heard air escaping lungs—mine and his. The gun smacked the sidewalk. Anya kicked it away. Where did she come from? I yelled, angry and too busy to kick her ass. "Get back in the car, dammit. Get back in the car."

I scrambled on top of the cabrón and wrestled him into submission with a choke hold. His kicking and biting subsided. I was too heavy. I looked up again, distracted by Anya's shadow. She stood over us. I squinted up at her. She bent to retrieve the pistol.

"I told you. Get back in the car. Don't you listen? I need you in the car."

I was breathing hard and panting. "Give me what you have in your hand, por favor."

"You're not going to kill him, are you?"

I looked at her coldly. "Why not? He wanted to kill us. Or did you think he was going to ask politely and wait for me to hand over the goodies for a thank you very much? Get back in the car and start the engine."

I cold-cocked cabrón with his own gun before handing it back to her. For good measure I pulled him around the corner of the bank and into a filthy alley. It amazed me in these places how quickly the atmosphere could change. I walked through shards of shattered glass to get to the car. Anya walked in front of me. She held the handgun at waist level.

"Let that thing drop to your thigh," I instructed. "No one will notice it there."

She did as she was told and we carried on to the car.

"Let's go. Drive." I checked the back seat. The bag was still there. "The reason I wanted you to stay with the car was because of the bag in the back seat," I explained, exasperated.

"Are we going to the panga, or the next bank?" she asked.

Good question. My decision came in a split second. "Panga. If we don't make the last bank, we can get away with what we've got. Don't forget to unload your shopping expedition, okay? I don't want to listen to you complain all the way home about how I cheated you out of your new wardrobe."

She was getting the hang of shifting. I gave it up and let her work the transmission, too, while I jerked back and forth in the passenger seat. I couldn't help laughing.

"How's my driving, Jimmy?" she wanted to know.

"Hand your phone over and let me call 1-800-EAT-SHIT. I'll leave a message for you."

She looked across at me and made her eye-rolling as obvious as she could. "Thanks. I think."

"Eyes on the road, woman. I don't want to die screaming and clawing for the door handle just yet."

FORTY-SIX

Getting to the panga was a piece of cake. The harbor was only two streets away. Anya struggled with the steering and the gas pedal. The car squealed around corners. A light turned red. She tramped on the brakes and screeched to a halt. She forgot to push in the clutch. The car died.

I scanned the road behind us. I looked from right to left. Nothing. The light turned green. Anya turned the key and started the car. Our getaway began with popping the clutch and burning rubber. The process started all over again. Every time Anya reached for the parking brake I grabbed her hand and placed it on the shifter, where it belonged.

"Kind of a spiteful wench, aren't you? You're doing that on purpose because it's Dulce's car."

She didn't answer. She was busy driving—if you could call it that. I didn't dare open my mouth again when I recognized the look of concentration glued to her freckled face. The wrinkled forehead gave it away.

"There. Turn there. It's the dock. Park here. Park here. Let's go. Let's get unloaded."

She opened the door and put a foot out. The car

drifted toward the water. I reached across for the brake and yanked it. The car shuddered and the engine quit. For good measure I grabbed the keys from the ignition. "Come on. Move your teenage ass, girl. We don't have a lot of time."

We scrambled onto the wooden wharf loaded with paper bags and the suitcase filled with cash. I scanned the wharf for our panga. Something wasn't right. I called to her. "Wait. There's someone on our panga. Wait here."

I pulled the pistol from my belt and kept it low against my leg. Whoever it was— "What the? Where did she come from? Bring the stuff. It's okay."

Reynaldo, the wharf rat. He was deep in conversation with someone I recognized.

Anya recognized her too. "Jimmy. It's Luz. What's she doing here? How did she get here?"

Luz wore the AK across her back, the same way she greeted us south of Todos. I wasn't fooled. I was familiar with the way she carried it. If she had to she'd be able to ready it in a split second. I had no doubt there would be a round in the chamber.

Luz stopped talking and grinned and waved. "Jim. Anya. Buenos dios. You know my cousin Reynaldo already."

We shook hands, but I wasn't sure if I was supposed to be relieved or concerned. I heard of this brand of new militia. It was comprised mostly of children. Their parents were murdered by the cartels or the police or the military or all of them. Time and again, no one could be bothered or convinced to investigate. If there was an investigation, no fault was ever found. Bodies were mutilated beyond recognition or burned or both. Thirty thousand deaths a year were the norm. It was horrible.

The children learned the hard way. There was no one left to comfort them. No one to turn to for help. No one to be trusted. No one to take responsibility for the deaths of their parents and grandparents and brothers and sisters and cousins. Even their animals were destroyed.

And now they were here to help me. And Anya. I wasn't going to say no if I could help it.

"We have one more run to make, Luz. Do you think you can hold the fort for us?"

A toothy grin illuminated her face until she pulled up her bandana to cover it. "Si, Jim. I will hold for as long as you need."

The girl's voice might be high-pitched, but there was no doubt about her intent. I explained we had one more trip. Told her about dos cabrones and the Baja buggy following us around town. Let her know about their leader, Dulce.

"No problemo. That cartel puta and her pinche pendejos will find trouble for sure, Jim. You can trust me. You can count on me. You too, Anya."

She smiled and turned and boarded the panga. The AK rolled off her back and out of sight below the gunnel. "Reynaldo will keep an eye out and warn me. Si, Reynaldo?"

"Si, mi proma. No problema."

"He has to keep a low profile, though, Jim. We need him here in the city. Don't expect him to take up arms."

I looked her straight in the eye and nodded. "No problemo, Luz. Te entiendo."

I motioned to Anya. Together we hurried back to Dulce's car.

"How come Luz can pronounce your name and Dulce couldn't?"

"Because Dulce was trying to seduce me and she thought I'd think it was cute."

"Only trying?"

My face turned a bright red, and it wasn't sunburn. "Never mind. Let's get going."

"Do you think by now Dulce's partners have found her?"

It was something I didn't want to consider. I should have left Anya with Luz. Except. I knew there was no way in hell she'd stay behind. If she wouldn't get on an airplane, she wouldn't wait for me at the panga. In other words, I was still baby-sitting, and not in a way I liked to do it with the danger she was in.

"Keep your eyes open," I told her. "I'll take us to the next bank, all right?"

She handed over the keys and climbed in beside me. "I want you to cover your face with a bandana, just like Luz, okay?"

Anya did as she was told. There was not a word of complaint from her lips.

FORTY-SEVEN

I hesitated before starting the car. I owed Anya an explanation, at least. "I've had dealings down here before, years ago, on the mainland. Vigilantes or self-defense forces. In Spanish, autodefensas. They formed up to combat a cartel in several of the towns. They had moderate success. In fact, their success brought them to the attention of the government.

"That's good, right?"

"Yes. Well, it was. The autodefensas had their own arms. They formed into groups. They kept tight control on communications so it couldn't be discovered who they were. Even their leaders didn't know any names."

I started the car and proceeded through the parking lot.

"They began having so much success compared to the local and state police and military forces that it started to make those guys look bad. Real bad. The politicians couldn't have that. The legal harassment started. Leaders were imprisoned. Arms were confiscated. The autodefensas are no more because they were interfering with the cartels."

"That's horrible."

"Yes it is. And thus we have children like Luz and Reynaldo and others taking up arms. They're having some success too, like the autodefensas. Somehow I doubt that they'll give up their arms this time. They know from experience. They have nothing else to lose. When everything you have is desaparecido, what else is there?"

I took us out of the marina parking lot and made for the last banco. Three for three would make it a very good day. "When I park, get in the driver's side and wait. Don't shut down, okay?"

"You still want me to drive?" She sounded doubtful.

"You bet. You're a natural stick-girl."

"Oh Jeem. Gracias."

"All right. That's enough of that. I can still put you over my knee—"

She interrupted me real quick. "You can try."

I laughed at the absurdity and closed the door. Looked in every direction. Didn't see anything out of the ordinary, whatever that meant with a street full of hung over gringos wandering aimlessly in the heat. There wasn't even a whisper of a breeze beneath the overcast to blow away the stink.

I looked off to the south. It was black as hell. When that storm hit, it would be every man for himself. If we got out of here in time we'd be lucky. I was glad Reynaldo had fueled us up on our arrival. I stuck my head in the window. Anya pulled down her bandana and smiled across at me before pulling it up. She looked more confident than I felt.

"Here we go. Keep an eye out, woman."

I made for the banco door. It was just like the first two times. I showed my passport. A form slid across the desk. I filled it out. The official gave it a cursory glance before leading me to the vault. I turned a matching key in the door. The official departed to leave me alone. I slid out the steel box and dumped the remainder of my money into the bag.

There it was. The last of the loot. I was home free and well on my way to owning my office building in Magic City. Maddie was going to be so happy.

I whistled tunelessly and strolled nonchalantly through the banco and out the open doorway clutching the carry-on. Anya waited patiently in the car. In the distance a dune buggy's throaty exhaust pipes assaulted the tourist throngs. It wasn't unusual.

Except.

Except the roar grew louder, and with the streets crowded with pedestrians, that would be a near impossibility. Or would it? "Let's go. I think I hear your amigos again."

"Why are they always my friends?" she wanted to know.

"Because you're the one that introduced yourself on the beach in that unique way you have of meeting new people."

Her brow furrowed and she floored the accelerator. She popped the clutch and the transmission groaned. Tires screeched and we were off. I jerked back and forth like a hula dollie stuck on a dashboard. I grabbed for the dash and braced myself.

"Your driving skills are excellent," I reassured her. "You should try convincing your mother to get you one of these for kicks."

"Yeah, right. Like that will ever happen. Now stop talking. I'm trying to drive."

"I can tell."

"No backtalk," she informed me. "We don't have time." She rolled her eyes.

Anya was starting to grow on me. I leaned over and reached for the mirror.

"You checking for leftover lipstick?"

I adjusted it to give a view behind us. Satisfied and exasperated at the same time, I turned to her. "Smartass."

"Just doing my job."

"What's that?" I wanted to know. There was something coming. With her, there always was.

"My job seems to be dragging you up by your bootstraps and keeping you on the straight and narrow."

I was in no position to disagree. "You might have to up your game a little." I turned away and looked out the window. I didn't want her to see the smile.

"I know, Jimmy. I'm working on it."

FORTY-EIGHT

Anya steered into the wharf's parking lot with tires squealing. She braked to a screeching halt. Switched off the ignition. The car jerked ahead before stopping. Relieved, I stopped bracing against the dash and sighed.

"I'm glad that's over with," she said.

She wasn't the only one. I opened the door and stood. I needed a look around. We weren't out of the woods yet. "Stay here. Don't open the trunk until Reynaldo or Luz show up."

"What? Why? Are you sure? I don't see anyone."

"Listen. Hear that?" How could she miss the roar of a Baja buggy getting closer? I changed my mind. We needed to get on the road right now.

"It's them. Come on. Open the trunk. We have a boat to launch and water to cross."

I looked up at the growing blackness. The wind was down. Water in the bay was calm, almost mirror-like. A darker color reflected from the overcast. We had to get out while the getting was good.

Anya thought different. "The weather is perfect. No wind. And the water is like glass. Our boat is going to fly."

"It's the calm before the storm. Look up and look south. We've got a couple of hours at most to hustle out of Dodge and get north. Go get the cart."

She ran off and I proceeded to unload the trunk. Outside of the money there were more bags and boxes than I had time to count. Anya returned pushing the cart. Luz walked with her. I smiled and wondered if she called shotgun with the AK. I nodded and we went to work loading our treasures.

Luz leaned into the car and pulled the keys. "That puta will not need her car." She tossed them into the water.

We looked at each other and we understood. I nodded in the direction of Anya and shook my head. "No problemo, Jim."

Anya managed to stuff everything from Dulce's car into the cart.

"Are you sure you don't want to do another shopping expedition? There might be something you missed. You know, like hanging around in that bar?"

"No Jimmy. I'm all done shopping. There's Sol in the cooler, remember?"

Luz perked up. "Yes, señor Jim. I checked. I added a few things since I'll be coming along for the ride home."

I wondered what that meant, but it wasn't the time to be asking. "All right. Let's go."

We were too late. Dulce and her compadres were edging up to the car. All three were armed, and the arms were aimed at us.

"Luz, take Anya to the boat. I'll handle this."

I reached behind my back for the automatic. My hand came up empty. "Shit."

They were coming at us fast, running. The expression on Dulce's face wasn't good. She was pissed. Her partners in crime weren't looking all that pleased either. "Where do you think you're going, Jim." There it was. Dulce wasn't trying to seduce me now. "You have what we want. Turn it over and we can go."

A gun exploded. Lead shattered the car's window. I looked around. Where the hell was Anya? I made for the car and crouched behind it and there she was. "I told you to get your ass out of here and onto the boat."

"I must have misheard. Are we going to be killed?"

"What did you do with my handgun?"

She reached into her bag and pulled it out.

"Dammit woman, that's no place for a gun.

"Well it's where I keep it."

All I needed now was for her to pout. "I'll spank you later."

"Like hell you will. You're going to be busy getting us out of this, this predicament."

I called out to Dulce. "Let the girl go. She has nothing to do with this."

"It's too late. She's going to die for pistol whipping me."

I looked at Anya. "Life's consequences are a bitch, aren't they?"

The look of fear on her face shut me up.

"Anya."

She wouldn't look at me. Instead, she stared slack-jawed at Dulce. If I didn't know better she was about to stand up. I made a grab for her arm. I tightened my grip and kept her down. For good measure I slapped her face with my other hand.

"Anya. Listen. Do not move from here. Under any circumstance. Until these cartel flunkies are down and done. Do you hear?"

She nodded, but she wasn't listening. She'd taken Dulce's threat to heart. She was convinced she was going to die.

A single shot rang out. It was loud and powerful. An AK. I looked toward the panga. Luz. Her face was concealed by the bandana. She was intent on making her way to us. The AK was tucked into her shoulder. For a tiny wisp of a girl, she knew how to handle it. She was so close I heard the fire control lever click. She was on full auto.

"Check out Luz, girl. See how she holds that rifle?" It was too late. Anya wasn't paying attention.

I waited for the burst. When it came, my plan was to grab Anya and drag her to the panga. "Come on!. Neither of us wants to come between Luz and Dulce now."

I grabbed her wrist. Luz called out. Her voice was clear and distinct. It wasn't a yell. It was measured. It was effective. For me, at least. I knew what was coming. I wondered if Dulce and her crew did.

"Pinche cartel de drogas puta." The AK began spitting lead under the capable hands of Luz. Brass clinked and bounced and scattered across parking lot asphalt. The firing halted. Luz got down to make a smaller target while she flipped the taped magazine. Split seconds later, she was firing and advancing toward us yet again. I hauled Anya down the wharf in the direction of the panga.

The muzzle of the AK came up and Luz handed us ski masks.

"Put these on. Both of you." I did as I was told. Anya wasn't so sure. She held out a shaking hand. I slapped it away and forced the mask over her head. She balked and fought me until her eyes found the holes.

"I don't like being blind."

"Better blind than dead, girl. Now get your ass behind me and Luz."

The AK fire halted. Luz was out of ammunition. I brought up my automatic and returned fire. Luz fitted another jungle mag into the AK. Where the hell did she keep them? I fired in short bursts, knowing I couldn't keep it up. To my relief Luz began backing up, protecting our six as she followed us down the wharf.

"I think they're down, Luz. There's no return fire. Let's go now. Did Reynaldo get away?"

She nodded. "It is good you put on the masks. There are too many amateurs with their phones. We must go now. The police will be here soon."

In the distance sirens sounded, growing louder and closer. I hopped into the panga and fired her up. Three engines and a thousand horsepower idled and echoed off the sides of the yachts moored on either side. Luz tossed the ropes and waved. She picked up the AK and stood guard with the AK on her hip. A third banana clip found its place.

I advanced throttles slowly to reverse the panga out of the berth. There was no one looking down on us from the mega-yachts. We had the wharf to ourselves.

Luz kept watch until I had the go-fast pointed at the ocean. She knew what was coming when she gripped the gunnel and moved to hang on. I powered up a thousand horsepower of go-fast engines and we were gone. We were headed for open water.

It felt like forever, but I made it past the break and we were home free. In the bottom of the panga, Anya lay shivering. I looked at Luz and nodded and she moved to comfort her. I don't know what she said, but Anya smiled and then laughed and all of a sudden they were in deep conversation. I had no clue how they could hear each other over the roar of the engines doing what they were built to do.

FORTY-NINE

We weren't out of it yet. Luz knew it, and I knew it. I wasn't certain Anya did. She interrupted my thoughts when she chose that moment to lean across and yell over the roar of the engines. Right away I noticed her hands traveling over parts of the cockpit in an attempt to steady herself. We were out of the protection of the harbor and rounding the cape into open sea. The panga rocked and rolled as it cut through the water at high speed.

"Luz thinks I'm your mistress."

"So that's what you two were laughing at. I noticed it took your mind off our firefight."

"Yeah. I set her straight. Now she thinks you're my father."

"There's no harm in that. It solves everything so far. Just remember, Anya. She put her own and her cousin's life on the line to help us. Don't lie to her about any of the big things."

In that instant I saw her looking more somber than at any other time. What I said must have jarred her. "You're right. I should have known. I'm an American teenager living a life of comfort. It didn't occur to me."

"Tighten it up, sailor. You're learning. That's what's important."

She nodded and I went on. "Why don't you take over as captain. You can show Luz what you've made of. If you do it right, she'll probably ask questions. You can show her what you know."

"Do you think I should?"

"Of course you should, sailor. It's her boat as far as we're concerned. She only loaned it out to us. If you can teach her about the nav system or anything else, go to it. She'll appreciate it, I'm certain."

Anya grinned and nodded and there was no holding her back. She motioned to Luz and the two of them broke into animated conversation. Anya's fingers danced over the electronics. I recognized the nav screen she pulled up. She changed position in front of the display and made room for Luz to take over the helm.

For the next while I knew the topic of conversation would concern the operation of the boat's electronics. To think I once considered Anya's presence a babysitting job didn't enter my mind now. She was well on her way to graduating into something and someone I didn't know.

I took a look at the sky. What I saw concerned me even more than it did in Cabo. In all directions, dark black clouds covered the horizon. We were headed north. It looked like we would be heading into the unknown.

A small door near the cockpit floor lead into the bow of the panga. I bent to open it. I felt for a switch and flipped it. The compartment flooded with a dull neon light from front to back. I transferred the cash followed by our baggage.

I was about to close the door when the corner of a drab green box caught my eye. I must have dislodged a tarp when I tossed the heavy cash-filled carry-on into the compartment. I took a closer look. There was more than one tarp. All of them looked to be arranged to conceal something.

I struggled to turn around. I looked for Luz. She was busy with Anya and the boat's command center. I closed the door and got down on my hands and knees before crawling into the narrow space separating the boxes. One at a time I gathered the covers and slid them off.

The markings were familiar, and I knew enough about them not to ask questions. I readjusted the covers and retreated. I turned off the light and closed the door. I looked to Luz in the cockpit, but she was still busy at the controls. She didn't notice the intrusion.

I put my back against the console and pushed myself upright. I wanted to keep an eye on our tail. My concern was another go-fast that might have been keeping an eye on the marina, watching for our departure. I checked my watch. We were a good thirty minutes out. The sky was getting blacker and the wind was picking up. Whitecaps blew across our path. The crests between swells were getting higher.

"Can you keep us between swells, Luz?"

She nodded knowingly. Anya wanted to know why.

"This thing is made of fiberglass for a reason. The only metal is the three engines. Any radar looking for us won't be able to pick us up. If we stay between swells as best we can we might not be spotted by a patrol boat."

"But won't we have to cross over as we get closer to shore?"

"Yes, but the time will be minimal overall. If we're lucky."

Anya didn't ask why a patrol boat would be looking for us. I didn't elaborate. They wouldn't be searching for us because of the shoot-up and the killings at the marina. By now the crooked police and military would be on the lookout for a gabacho and his crew stupid enough to deal a bad hand in public to cartel worker drones. I'd bet the word was out and the reward would be substantial.

That we were probably on the run in a former cartel go-fast appropriated by a bunch of kids with plans to put up a fight wouldn't be good, either. Who else could afford an extravagant panga outfitted with the latest in cockpit technology and engine power? I called to Luz and asked.

The girl nodded furiously. Her lips moved, and I could barely make out what she was saying over the roar of the engines and the wind. "Si, Jim. It is."

She steered us onto the crest of a swell, and I wondered if she was trying to distract me. I looked back, a quick look. It confirmed my worry. There was another go-fast behind us. It churned up a huge wake. That told me it was more powerful than ours. It would most likely overtake us.

We topped a second crest. Another hurried look revealed two boats, and then nothing as Luz steered us to the trough's bottom. We needed to get farther offshore if we were going to outrun both pangas. If. A big if.

I motioned to Luz. She was busy at the controls while Anya continued to demonstrate the capabilities of the nav system. I got Anya's attention and she poked Luz.

I held up two fingers and pointed aft. She nodded. Immediately she cranked the wheel and we were at ninety degrees to the swell. She didn't touch the throttles. The panga plowed through the crests, one at a time. The engines found air. Grabbed it. Roared in complaint. Then caught and grabbed more sea to propel us through the next. Half a dozen waves later we settled into a trough.

Through it all, Anya dropped to the deck and was hanging on for dear life to anything that was tied down. I bent over her. She shook uncontrollably. Tears rolled down her face. She was terrified.

"It's all right now. We'll be fine. We're in the trough. We'll be in this one for a while. I wanted to warn you but I didn't have time."

She swiped at her eyes. "Is this what you meant by tighten it up? If it is, every part of my body is tight. Even some that weren't meant to be."

I roared with laughter. Even Luz heard me over the engines. She turned to look.

"You're going to be all right, sailor," I told her. "Now stand up and we'll wave fists at our pursuers."

The go-fasts behind us looked to be gaining. Either they followed us from Cabo, or saw us cresting the swells and wanted to know who it was. My bet was the latter.

Cell-phone calls must have confirmed we were an unknown quantity.

I gestured to Luz and she looked, but already it was too late. Our pursuers descended into their own trough. In five or ten minutes we would end up dangerously close to shore.

"We're going to have to crest half a dozen to get some distance to our next run, Luz."

Luz gestured for me to take the wheel. She moved past Anya in the cramped cockpit. I nudged Anya out of the way while my eyes roamed over the instruments. Eighty knots indicated and this thing was no slouch with a thousand horsepower's worth of engines deafening all of us. My eyes halted at a switch. It said Plane.

Of course. All this money for a boat. It had to have a plane. Over the course of a couple of minutes I varied the settings. Our speed fell off a couple of knots, and I knew that wasn't right. I tried the other direction. Fiddled with it while watching our speed. Managed to gain three more knots. The engines held us at eighty-three, tops. We were on the plane, and she would go no faster.

Anya launched a flurry of punches at my shoulder. "Where's Luz? Jim? She's not here."

<h1>FIFTY</h1>

I knew where Luz was. Did I want to alert Anya? Did she need to know we were in danger? Up to now she'd been a real trouper, but that would be a whole different scenario for her to process, and I was concerned for her. That concern would have to wait, though. Luz beckoned to me from the crawlspace I visited earlier.

"When I make a sign, if you are able, you must hand me what I have prepared," she instructed.

"I'm not so certain about that. Anya is on edge. I'm not sure she's going to be able to handle much more of this."

Luz pointed to a smaller compartment just beneath the gunnel. "Look in there."

I hauled out two life jackets. They weren't the old Mae West style, either. They were brand new. If they went into the water they would inflate automatically. There was a strobe light attached. I helped Luz into one and helped her secure it before taking the other. I nudged Anya and handed her the life jacket. I took over piloting the panga.

"I'll help you put it on. Luz has one already," I said. I made sure to fasten it securely and snugged it around her.

I tugged at it fore and aft and sideways. It didn't budge. When I was satisfied I did the same for Luz.

"Is that where she's been? Finding these?"

"Probably." I told her it would inflate automatically. I pressed the test button. The strobe flashed. She looked at Luz, before looking down at her jacket. I already knew what she was thinking.

"Where's yours, Jimmy?"

"There's only two," I admitted. "You and Luz get first dibs."

"But but—"

"No buts about it. You need to know I was a first-class college swimmer back in ye olden days." It was only a bit of a fib. I couldn't swim a stroke.

The panga chose that moment to shudder as the bow took a wave and disappeared for a split second. Anya screamed.

"I'll take the wheel. You help Luz, okay? It's your job to do whatever she tells you. Understood, sailor?"

Water splashed. The fastboat shuddered. She nodded, eyes wide, her face pale.

"No questions, Anya. I know you can do it."

She said yes loud enough for me to hear. I leaned into Luz and let her know Anya would be her second. Luz nodded and produced a coil of nylon rope. She handed me an end and I tied it off on a gunnel cleat using a bowline. She stretched the rope across the cockpit to the opposite gunnel and pulled it snug before tying it off. The jackline was secure.

I heard her tell Anya to hang on tight, no matter

what. That was the last I saw of Luz as she disappeared into the bow of the panga. Anya looked after her and yelled into the void. "Do you need any help?"

The answer must have been no, because Anya looked in my direction and shrugged. I motioned for her to come to me. She hung onto the jackline Luz rigged up for her and crossed the panga.

"Luz will be busy for a few minutes. Don't worry. She knows what she's doing and she's experienced at it. I suspect she's been doing it for a while."

Anya nodded.

"Do what she says when she says it and we'll all be good, okay, sailor?"

"I'm not feeling like much of a sailor right now, Jim."

"Come on, woman. Tighten it up." I grinned at her and she returned a nervous smile. "That's the spirit." I wrapped an arm around her shoulders and gave her an encouraging hug just as a wave crashed down on us. I let go to grab the wheel.

"See that button?" I pointed. The label said Bilge.

"Flip it on. A light should show it's working. If it doesn't, we're both going to have to bail this tub."

Anya yelled at me. "Are you for real?"

I should have known better. "No. But be sure to let me know if the light goes out, okay?" I put an arm around her a second time and pulled her close. She had both hands welded to the jackline.

"I can't tie you to the jackline Luz rigged for you. If we flip, you won't get out from under it. All you can do is use it to steady yourself. Understood?"

FIFTY-ONE

Anya collapsed and slipped slowly to her knees. I should have known better than to tell her she'd have to swim for it. "Come on, woman. Keep it tight."

That got her. I knew it would. She made a grab for the jackline and pulled herself up with one hand. She made a fist and banged my shoulder hard with the knuckles of the other.

"Good one. You've definitely got a brother." I removed a hand from the wheel and rubbed at what I knew would soon turn into a bruise. I was glad to see she was still feisty. "That's my girl. Now take the wheel. I need to help Luz."

"Help her do what?" she wanted to know.

Wait and learn, but I didn't say word one. I pretended not to hear. I didn't have time to explain. And even if I did, Anya wouldn't comprehend it anyway.

Luz disappeared into the bow. I knew what she was going for. I'd already seen it. It would have been my first choice, too. If she wanted to rain down hellfire and brimstone, that would be the weapon of choice. She stuck her head out and waved me in. "I need your help.

You must protect Anya. I am not sure what she will do when she sees this."

"Not a problem, but there is one thing, Luz."

The look of determination on her face revealed everything. Whatever it was, it wouldn't faze her in the slightest. "What's that?"

"We're going to have to slow down. We need to be close to them for success."

"No problemo, Jim. I will need you to support me with the AK. Have you loaded any of those tracer rounds?"

"Yes. Anya did. I checked her work. It's good. I'll tell her."

I explained to Anya what we needed. She looked at me like I was crazy. "You want me so slow down? They're gaining on us. I know, because I looked over my shoulder. When you were busy. They're catching up." She was on the verge of panicking again.

"Exactly. We need them to catch up to us. They have to be close so we can take them out."

She kept busy wrestling with the wheel, attempting to keep the panga in the trough, but I could almost see her own wheels turning. "Take them out? You mean— What do you mean?"

"No. We're going to neutralize their boat. It's that or swim. Are you up to swimming in this ocean?" What else could I tell her? I wasn't going to admit anything else. She'd have to figure it out on her own.

"I'm going to help Luz. Slow it down to 50 knots or so, okay?"

Her body language said she didn't want to do it, but the revs went down and the panga lurched as it settled into the trough with reduced speed. Luz called my name and I bent to retrieve the rocket. I loaded, twisted, and she was good to go.

I called to Anya. "Keep it in the trough. Just like this."

I was pretty sure the panga on our tail couldn't believe it's good fortune. Rounds hit the transom. If they managed to score an engine, we'd be in the shit. I shouldered the AK and fired a quick burst. Then I remembered we needed them closer, and aimed over their heads. Luz called ready. I moved beside Anya.

"Get down. Now." I pushed her to the deck. "And stay down."

A loud whoosh and a bright flash announced the departure of the rocket. The boom as it hit the panga was louder. I high-fived Luz and ordered Anya to hit the throttles.

"What happened? What was that light?" Her eyes were squeezed closed. Just as well.

"We just sent our pursuers a message."

I looked back. Panga numero uno was dead in the water in more ways than one. Number two was holding off, but Luz wasn't discouraged.

"Load," she told me.

I did as I was ordered. Inserted and twisted. Hit her shoulder. Luz raised the weapon for a second time and tucked it into her shoulder. She aimed and the second whoosh announced the rocket's departure for watery pastures. The whump wasn't as loud, but Luz had found her mark again.

"They'll drown. Are we going back for survivors?" Anya asked.

I considered for a moment. I wanted Anya to take the time to figure out what she had asked. I decided not to wait. "No. They were out to kill us. We did ourselves a favor. Thank Luz and your lucky stars that girl knows what she's doing. Power up and get us out of here."

She hesitated, looking at me for just a little too long. I didn't feel bad. I didn't feel guilty. Todos Santos wasn't far away now, and getting up the Baja and across to home in the van would be a cakewalk compared to this.

FIFTY-TWO

Anya hit the throttles. Three engines roared and the fastboat jolted forward with a thousand horsepower hanging off the transom. It hit its stride and ended up on the step in jig time without having to adjust the trim. Whoever had set this thing up did a pretty good job, given its intent. I checked the console. It showed 83 knots.

"How far to go, Anya?"

Anya punched the screen with a finger, slid it around, and called up the display. "Wait. Start over and show Luz, okay? It's her boat. She needs to know this stuff. You and I will never see it again."

While Anya and Luz busied themselves with the navigation system, I had time to notice our surroundings. The sky was brightening to the north. The sun was peeking out, warming the cockpit considerably.

Was I safe in assuming we were outrunning the hurricane? I stripped off my jacket and tossed it aside. It was definitely warming. The sea was calming, too. We were no longer a cork bobbing on the Pacific Ocean. I looked over at the women. They were intent on the console. I smiled, satisfied and pleased Anya finally got it.

I watched them fuss and chatter and laugh and thought how fortunate we were now that our pursuers were finished. I edged up to the girls and called to Anya over the triple engine roar.

"That place we stopped for a swim is still ahead of us, right?"

She nodded and pointed at the map.

"We could hole up there and take a break. Maybe beach this thing and you two could have a swim if you want. It's warmer ashore and that water was nice and fresh."

Two heads huddled and put mouths to ears and then looked over at me and nodded. Great. "I'll check the cooler while you two freshen up."

Anya's eyes flashed and she managed to get in an eye-roll. Luz gave her the elbow and bent to say something I couldn't hear. They broke out laughing and I figured, teenagers. Female teenagers. I was smart enough to know I knew nothing about them.

Luz cut the throttles and hit the switch to tip the engines out of the water. The silence was deafening. She ran the panga onto the beach like an expert. The girls high-fived. I threw out the anchor and hauled it ashore.

Anya handed off the cooler and I carried it to our firepit. Wind-flattened Baja buggy tracks surrounded our old campsite. I figured the cabrones must have got brave after we departed and came back for a look-see. They wouldn't have seen much with Anya and her AK long gone by then. I smiled to myself remembering the sight of her aiming it at them without a magazine and then forgot about it as the women jumped ashore.

Luz had her AK over her back and the one she'd given me strung over a shoulder. She handed it to me and looked me straight in the eye. "You will be our lookout. Understand, Jim?"

"Si, Luz. I will follow your orders."

Even so, she kept her AK and the two of them headed off to the freshwater pond carrying Anya's shopping bags. I looked after them and wondered what would be coming back—not that it was any of my business. I was certain Luz could use some teenage time with another girl, unburdened with the realities of life lived under cartel dirty thumbs.

I dragged some good-sized driftwood to our firepit and rolled it on top of the smaller bits and pieces we left behind. I boarded the beached panga and collected the tarp and a jerry can of fuel. I wasted some on the wood and tossed a match. The wood ignited with a satisfying whump and an orange flash. I smoothed the tarp on the ground and opened the cooler.

An envelope lay on top of the contents, addressed to Luz, written in simple printing. I was tempted to open it, but my Spanish was at a kindergarten level at best. Instead, I put it aside and wondered who it was from.

To kill time I investigated the contents of the cooler.

A Sol for Anya. Check. Burritos. Check. Water. Check. I placed the tinfoil-covered burritos at the edge of the fire. They'd be nice and warm by the time the women returned.

Flames bit into the biggest pieces of driftwood and before long they began crackling and popping. I pulled the tarp back from the flames before picking up the AK and walking around the campsite. I glanced in the general direction of the pond, not wanting the women to think I was spying on them. I had orders from Luz, after all, and I wasn't going to disobey.

I made my way back to the fire and propped the AK against the cooler. In minutes the high-pitched voices of the women made their way to the warmth of the fire. The little devils settled on the tarp and looked up at me with raised eyebrows.

"What's with your mouth, Jimmy?" Anya asked.

I finally remembered to close it before responding. "Uhh. What? You two—"

"We clean up pretty good, don't we, Jimmy?"

The girls high-fived and I used the opportunity to roll the hot burritos away from the fire with a stick.

"Dinner is served. If you don't see something, all you have to do is ask." I handed Anya her beer.

"Thanks, Jimmy." She popped the top on the edge of the cooler and moved to hand it off to Luz. She shook her head. "I do not drink. A water please, Jim."

I already had it out for her. I took one too. We marveled at the warm food and cool drinks, and then our mouths were too busy chewing to waste time talking.

Once again, Anya impressed me. Who would have known this was the same teenager I picked up in La Paz? Mind you, La Paz was a lifetime away now, for both of us.

I allowed my mind wander to thoughts of home and what Maddie might be doing. For sure she'd have murder on her mind when I showed up—if not right this very minute. I sighed and bit into the burrito and tried not to think about it.

FIFTY-THREE

We were packing up to leave. The cooler was closed. The tarp folded.

"Are we going to put the fire out?" Anya asked.

"No. I'm going to throw more wood on it. If anyone is on the lookout for us, they'll see the smoke. If we're lucky they'll think we're still here."

Luz thought it was a good idea, too. Anya and Luz added wood and stoked the fire while I carried our gear to the panga. The fire renewed itself with the fresh driftwood and smoke began billowing up into the still air. If anyone out on the ocean was looking for someone, it would be a good beacon.

The women helped load what was left of our gear, including the AKs and the snacks still in the cooler. I went back to collect the tarp and tossed it on the bow. Anya and Luz crossed the bow to the cockpit. The added stern weight raised the bow off the sand. I climbed aboard and huffed and puffed as I manhandled the heavy anchor aboard. When this adventure was over, Friday and I would be going on a diet and exercise routine— that is, if Maddie allowed me to keep living.

Luz switched on. Electric motors whined as the heavy

engines tilted into the ocean. She leaned and looked over the edge. Satisfied with the depth, she fired up an engine, allowing it to warm before reversing and advancing the throttle. She fired up two and three and set them to idle.

It was only a minute. It seemed like a lifetime before Luz warned us with a wave of a hand. I grabbed hold of Anya and gripped the jackline in order to brace for takeoff. There was no other word for it as a thousand horsepower confined to three outboard engines roared to deafening life. Propellers grabbed water and the panga jumped forward. In no time it was on the plane and indicating 83 knots. I know, because I checked.

Ahead of us in the distance off the port side, a cloud of black smoke poked its way over the horizon. It was no panga. I gestured to Luz and she nodded. I leaned into Anya and asked her to show me where the shoal would be ahead of us. She enlarged the display and pointed to it while explaining to Luz how it worked.

The black exhaust had to be a coast guard vessel. There was nothing else it could be. It would belong to Mexico or the United States, on patrol for drug runners. In this calm sea there'd be no hiding from its radar. I cupped my hands and yelled over the engines.

"We need to put that thing on a course for the shoal you marked. The tide is in. That will keep it hidden."

Was there a chance the patrol boat would be aware of our shoal? Slim to none, I figured. What was the chance we could lure it onto the shoal to disable it?

That was the half a million-dollar question. I had my doubts.

FIFTY-FOUR

I wondered aloud to Luz if the patrol boat might be coming for us. She motioned for Anya to take the controls. She glanced at the instrument panel and gave a thumbs up, impressing me no end.

"There is no doubt, Jim. The vessels have been operating in our waters for so many years."

"What will happen if it's Mexican?" I wanted to know.

Luz didn't hesitate. "If it is our boat, they will board us, if they don't shoot us out of the water. The cartels would not be happy to learn we sunk one of their boats. Only our firepower kept more away from us."

We were done for. "Let me talk to Anya."

Luz moved out of the way and I approached Anya. She was busy fiddling with the navigation system.

"Is there any way you can track the progress of that vessel?"

She looked up at me with shining eyes. Something was up. "I already have. The satellite system tracked its course. They should intercept us here." She ran her fingers over the display and a red X appeared.

"You did that? Where's the shoal?"

Anya moved her fingers to enlarge the view and the latitude and longitude location of the rock shoal came up. A cross-hair hovered over it.

"So that's it?"

"Yup. I know you're thinking something. What is it?"

Anya needed to know. Luz looked from me to Anya. She knew all too well what was coming up.

"We need to disable it."

"What? What do you mean, disable? You mean disable as in sink? You're crazy," Anya said.

"Exactly to both points."

"But what if it's one of our ships?"

"We still need to disable it, don't you think?" I didn't give her time to consider the effects of that on the crew. "We need to lure it over that rock to disable it. Can you do it?"

Now she was thinking. I could almost hear the wheels turning over the roar of the engines.

"Think about it. Mexican or American, it will have a cannon. And that cannon will be radar controlled. On flat water, it will pick up the engines. We'll be sitting ducks."

Luz grabbed Anya's arm and squeezed. "It is true, Anya. If it is one of our boats, our lives will be worth nothing. You do not know how it is with our military on the cartel payroll."

Anya consulted the display. The track line of the two vessels showed the intercept point to be past the underwater rock. The tide was in. There was no danger of the rock revealing itself with waves crashing on it as it had for us on our cruise past the rock.

The engines quieted only a little as Anya reduced throttle. A new intercept location showed. She slowed again and we waited for the screen to update.

"If we can get between the rock and shore and wait—"

"We have to keep our bow pointed toward them. You know. In case they open fire or something."

"Open fire? Luz?"

"I will not fire on a coast guard ship. Maybe it is American. They will take my boat. I can't do anything about that."

I suspected Luz was more concerned with the cargo we were carrying than the panga. I didn't blame her. But I didn't want her firing on one of ours, either. For some reason I couldn't picture myself locked up in an American brig. I didn't want to even consider a Mexican prison. "We'll have to take a chance."

"Jimmy? Will we go back to rescue the men?"

"Anya, they're sailors. On a big boat. They have lifeboats. They have lifeboat drills. They have life jackets. They probably know how to swim."

She thought about that.

"I don't want to end up in the brig with any of you," I added. As if that would happen.

FIFTY-FIVE

There was no way in hell we could run past the navy patrol vessel in front of us. Speed wasn't the consideration. We could easily outrun it. The problem was that it was on an intercept course. Even if we could make more speed, it wouldn't matter. The patrol boat was blocking our access to our drop-off south of Todos.

One option would be to turn back and make for Cabo. The trouble is, that wasn't in the cards following our shootout on the wharf. Another option would take us far out to sea. We could use our speed to outflank it. In that case, fuel became a consideration and we might not make our rendezvous point. We wouldn't look so good floating like a cork on the Pacific with dead engines.

There was only one alternative. "Make for the rock shoal. Bring us in as close as you can to shore without going aground."

Anya nodded. Luz's eyes never left the navigation screen. She was taking it in like a sponge soaking up Pacific seawater.

"Last chance ladies. We face it here, or we head back to Cabo in a hurry." And still run out of fuel before we got there, I didn't say.

"No, Jim," Luz said. "We know what is in Cabo. They will be waiting for us."

Anya nodded. "We shot the place up. We can't go back. We can't go back."

The panic in Anya's voice was obvious. Luz and I exchanged glances.

"You two make a good team. I agree. We can't go back."

That seemed to settle Anya a bit. I was proud of both of them. Luz was a natural. Anya was a quick learner, and a good teacher for Luz.

"You're going to have to keep the panga broadside. We need to be able to move fore and aft to keep the cruiser on course for the shoal. Can you do that?"

"Yes we can. We'll do it together, right Luz?"

They shrieked like banshees and began nattering back and forth like twins on a mission. They bent over the display and lost themselves in teacher and student.

Except.

Except this time it was a matter of life and death. I sensed the panga slowing as Luz delicately eased back the throttles. She slowed the engines to full stop and the panga slowed and halted. The coast guard vessel slowed, too. A crewman with binoculars manned the deck. Armed sailors lined the bow.

"Check the flag," I called. It was ours. I wondered if the navy sent bills to civilians for damages to property.

Anya screamed. "Back! Back up, Luz."

The warning came too late, if it was a warning. Luz had the panga positioned perfectly in a line with the patrol boat and the shoal. A loud screech announced the arrival of the coast guard vessel on the rocks. It shuddered before halting and slowly began tipping over on it's port side. The sailors on the bow scattered. The shoal held it at an angle of about ten or fifteen degrees. There would be no cannon fire in our future.

"Well, the good news is that it's not sinking. Let's get a move on before they launch a boat."

Luz took over the bridge. She advanced the throttles on the idling engines and we were off. A huge wake followed us until she got on the step, and in no time we were at speed. I kept a wary eye on the patrol boat. In minutes a hard-bottom with an armed crew came around the stern and made to chase after us. It was no match for our panga's three powerful engines. It wasn't capable of gaining ground on our thousand horsepower fastboat. The hard-bottom slowed and returned to the grounded ship.

Relieved, I turned to Luz. "How long?"

Luz consulted the screen. "We will be at our drop off south of Todos in half an hour.

I went below to prepare an AK for our beach party. Luz saw what I was doing and gave a thumbs up. I pointed at her AK. She grinned and nodded, knowing I would have it ready for her. Better to be prepared, in case our Baja buggy cabrones had amigos waiting for us in the dry riverbed.

Anya squatted down beside me and watched while I readied the AKs. "Do you think those will be necessary?"

I wanted to tell the truth, but at the same time, I

wondered if she needed it sugar-coated. "I don't know. Judging by the reception we got prior to our departure from Cabo, we need to be safe."

"Are you sure those will keep us safe?"

"This is all we have—as far as I know. I'm not privy to what other treasures Luz might have tucked away in the bow."

Anya shuddered. The panga changed course. The roar of the engines ceased as Luz cut the throttles and made for shore. I straightened. That's when I saw the second van on the riverbed. I racked the AK.

"Anya. Get down. Luz. There's two vans."

Luz held her hand out. "Do not be concerned, Jim. The van is for me. I will need your help to unload."

"That's no problem, Luz. You've got me for as long as you need."

She nodded. The silence was unreal but for the whine of the electric motors raising the engines out of the water as we drifted onto the beach.

"You want the anchor?"

Luz shook her head. "No. No time."

Luz was in a hurry to get away, too. I couldn't tell if our van was parked in the riverbed since we left. If it was, it was a dead giveaway, one that Anya and I didn't need now that we were back on solid ground.

"Was the van here the whole time, Luz?"

I was pretty certain it was going to be a problem if it was. Cosa the dog chose that moment to appear. Recognizing the voice of his mistress, he jumped up, barking and wagging his tail like there was no tomorrow, happy to have Luz home.

"No. I had dos compadres take care of it for you."

Even Anya heard my sigh of relief, and she was busy offloading the panga. Two men climbed on board to help unload the boxes Luz stashed in the panga's bow in Cabo.

"By land and sea both, Luz?"

"Yes, Jim. Sometimes we cannot depend on getting what we need overland. We must transport it into the ports. We do what we must."

I held up my hands. "I don't need to know more than that, Luz."

Anya was busy working up a sweat unloading our gear. "Jimmy, do you want this?" She held up the AK with both hands. I nodded in the affirmative, and she strapped it across her back exactly as I showed her.

Luz appeared impressed. "You trained her well, Jim. Did you show her how to shoot it also?"

"Yes I did. She might not be able to hit anything, but she knows how to load, fire, and clear."

"Those are the most important parts, for sure. We all must start someplace."

Anya dropped the suitcases off the panga's bow. I picked them up and hauled them to our van, and then called out to remind her to bring the ammo bag.

"I'll be right there, Jimmy."

Anya jumped off the bow and fell to her hands and knees. She gagged and caught her breath and threw up. I ran to her and knelt beside her. I took off my neckband and poured water on it before wiping her face.

"It's nerves. You'll be fine. You didn't have time to react with everything happening. The rough sea. The boats chasing us. All of it. You're okay now. You're safe."

I helped her up and she collapsed into my arms, still trembling and shaking. I eased her down onto the sand on her knees and motioned for Luz to join us. I moved away and listened while Luz explained what was happening.

"It is nerves. Everything that happened to us today is new to you. All of it." She halted and Anya nodded. "Jim and I have seen it before. For him, it is not so normal, yet he has experience."

Anya turned to look at me.

"For me, Anya, it is normal with the cartels closing in on us in this country. They kill everyone. Our parents. Our grandparents. Our bothers and sisters. Even our pets."

Anya's body drooped and uncontrollable sobbing overtook her yet again. "I'm so sorry you have to experience all of it, Luz. I'm sorry. I can't help you. I don't know what to do."

"You must allow Jim to take you home. Both of you must work together to do that. Just as you have worked to help me since we left Cabo San Lucas. That is your job now. To get each other home safe."

Anya nodded.

"I cannot help you any longer, Anya. It is up to the two of you now."

Luz helped the girl to her feet. They hugged and whispered and did things teenage girls do when they were friends. Whatever that was.

"You must take my dog to Todos for me," Luz said. "I have one last thing I must do."

I loaded the bags of money into the van along with Anya's new wardrobe. There wasn't much of it to load. Luz had been the beneficiary of a shopping spree courtesy of Anya. When it came down to it, Anya was a practical girl, and the clothes she bought for herself were common-sense. At least, they looked like it to me. No doubt Luz would at least wear some of them.

The girls hugged and cried and hugged again. I tried not to listen, but I couldn't help overhearing promises to stay in touch and text and send pictures and then they separated for the last time. Anya scooped up the dog and held the wiggling pile of hair.

"Are both of you coming with me or what?"

I ducked into the back of the van before I got an answer I didn't expect. I opened one of the money bags and dropped a gift for Luz in Anya's last remaining shopping bag. I carried it out and handed it off.

We hugged and Anya cried some more and hugged Luz again and I almost broke into tears too. If Maddie could only see me now.

Yeah, no. Not a chance. She'd kill me in a heartbeat when she got her hands on me.

FIFTY-SIX

I carried the weapons to the van and covered them beneath a blanket. It wouldn't hide anything in a thorough search. I hoped having Anya to distract the soldiers at the checkpoint would be enough. The soldiers were mostly teenagers themselves.

Luz didn't look in her gift bag right away. She tossed it up on the bow and climbed aboard and we helped push her out. She waited for the panga to drift into deeper water before lowering the engines. One by one they came to life with a familiar roar.

Luz bent, out of sight, and then straightened with a huge smile. She waved to us before giving an enthusiastic thumbs up. She yelled something. It sounded like Santiago, but by then she was too far out and I couldn't tell for sure.

The engines came to life as she firewalled the throttles. The fastboat steered north toward Todos Santos.

I walked with Anya to the van and gave it the once-over. Satisfied, I climbed in and turned the key. A huge explosion from out on the water echoed across the riverbed. I looked north and witnessed a small cloud of debris settling out of sight on the water.

"Jimmy—" Anya was panicking again.

"It's the boat. She had to get rid of it. There's nowhere to hide it. Not in these parts."

"Do you think she'll be all right?" Anya asked.

"It was always the plan, I'm sure. There's nothing else she could do, Anya. Luz will be fine, I promise. Why else would she ask you to take her dog to Todos for her?"

She didn't look convinced, but if things were reversed I most likely wouldn't be, either. Anya got in the van finally and I worked the heavy vehicle upstream in the dry riverbed. I angled it up and across the bank and we rocked and rolled north onto the paved two-lane highway. I passed the Baja buggy outfit without slowing. Anya frowned and crossed her arms as it disappeared from view in my side window.

"We're not stopping for anything? They had vending machines in that dune buggy place."

"We'll pick up supplies in Todos. I plan on driving non-stop to the border. Are you in?"

Anya rubbed her eyes and yawned. It was a long day for both of us and it wasn't over yet. It wouldn't be over until we crossed la frontera.

"I'll pick up a pillow. You can sleep on the way," I told her. "I'll see if I can find a foamy, too. It's going to be a long haul. It's going to be hot. And it's going to be dry and dusty."

She grimaced and gave me a fake smile.

"Are you still glad you didn't fly home?" I asked her.

"Of course. I'm having the adventure of my life. Well, except for the shootout on the dock. And the two boats we sank."

"Don't exaggerate. No one will believe you." That went over like a lead balloon. As if to emphasize it, the dog wriggled in Anya's arms and she put her down on the floor.

"We only sunk one boat," I explained.

"Who's this we you speak of, Jimmy?"

I considered for a moment. "It's all about perception. You might think we sunk two, but we only sunk one. We allowed the other one to stay afloat, remember? It got away, too."

That about covered it in my book. A Coast Guard vessel wasn't high on my priority list of sinking ships, especially when I was involved.

"We might have allowed it to float, but the last time I saw it, it was just sitting there, looking all dejected and half on its side. Kind of like that Italian tour boat in the Mediterranean, remember?"

"Oh come on. Our boat was smaller than a cruise liner. It was a coast guard ship. No tourists on board."

She looked at me like I was nuts.

"Si?"

She shrugged and we high-fived and that ended the discussion. We were coming up on Todos, and Anya was beginning to get antsy. She squirmed in her seat and leaned into the dash to look out the window.

"You're not keeping Luz's dog. I won't allow it. It's her dog. You can't have Luz on your six, searching for her dog. Remember the job she did for us on that Cabo wharf?"

"I wouldn't think of it, Jimmy."

I didn't know if she meant the shootout, or having Luz on her six. She sat back and seemed to relax, but I new she was probably thinking about how she could sneak the dog past me. She bent to retrieve the dog from the floor and placed her on her lap. The dog sat there, staring out the window. Probably waiting for Todos Santos to arrive when she'd get to see her mistress again.

"Look. There's the market."

I pulled off the street and parked. Already it was hot and humid. I looked up at the dark sky following us north. So far, we were still ahead of the looming storm.

"I'll wait while you get us some food, okay? We can't leave what's in the van all by itself. Comprende? And put the nice puppy down, okay?"

"Si, señor."

The sun was beating down. The heat was beginning to get unbearable. I got out of the van and began pacing. Worried. Where the hell was that woman now? Had she run off or been kidnapped? I gave her another two minutes. She appeared in one, coming around the corner. She worked to push a shopping cart. It was no mean feat, considering the obstacles she had to run those wheels over. I rushed to pull on the cart. Bags of food and ice and a cooler and fresh fruit ended up in the back of the van.

"I'll make us something to eat while you drive, okay?"

How could I say no to that? We were both starving.

"One more stop," I told her. "The foamy, remember? I'll get sheets and a couple of pillows, too."

Anya had lunch ready by the time I returned with the mattress and sheets. "Did you get a pillow? I need a pillow."

Considering what the girl had just been through, I figured another couple of minutes wouldn't hurt. She seemed pleased when I returned and pulled a pillow case onto the pillow. I set up the foamy in the back and covered it with the sheet and placed the pillow at the top.

"There ya go, girl. All the comforts of the modern world, just for you."

I thought she was going to start crying again, but she turned away and looked out her side window. I steered the van out of the lot and we ate on the run. She didn't complain once about having to wipe my chin when I was too busy avoiding potholes with one hand while clutching a ham and lettuce with generous mayo and mustard in the other.

"How are you feeling?"

"About having to wipe your chin like you're a geriatric old man?"

"If you're telling me I'm an old man, then you're an old woman. No. How do you feel about driving for a while? Until it gets dark, maybe?"

FIFTY-SEVEN

I didn't take time to explain the hazards of driving on a Mexican highway at night to Anya. Why would I? It was broad daylight. I asked her to wake me before it got dark, and she said sure, and that was that. I climbed into the back. I didn't need to picture myself stretched out on the foamy. It was right in front of me. I remarked on how nice it was to have a pillow before I whacked it into submission.

"Yeah, don't forget to thank me very much, sailor."

I stretched out on the mattress with a loud sigh. Maybe I was putting too much on Anya after her experience on the Cabo wharf and the panga. Maybe she was the one who needed the sleep.

Except. She was a teenager. When did they need to sleep? Didn't teenagers party all weekend long and go back to school or work or whatever they did with their time? I was pretty sure there was something I needed to explain. Something. What was it again? I didn't care any more. I couldn't fight sleep. The explaining would have to wait. I dropped off into la-la land like an conditioner falling out a window.

The air conditioner smashed into the ground so hard it woke me up. I opened an eye. It was pitch black inside the back of the van. An outline of someone in the open sliding door rustled furtively, oblivious to my presence. I squinted through both eyes, made a grab for an ankle, and tugged, hard.

Something solid smacked against the side of the van and a body landed on top of me. I pushed him off and heard a female voice.

"Damn it, Jimmy. It's me. Anya. Remember? Wake up, you sleeping dog."

"Sorry. I'm sorry. Open a darned door and let some light in."

"The door is open. It's night," she informed me.

"What? What the hell? You were supposed to wake me."

"You were snoring so loud you couldn't hear me calling your name. But we're stopped now. You're welcome to take over."

"What are you doing back here?" I wanted to know.

"Looking for the jack."

"What? The jack? What for?"

"Yeah, I hit something going 80 miles an hour," she said.

"And now you want to kill it?"

"No, silly. I want to change the tire," she said. "We have a flat."

Shit." I was wide awake now.

"Wait a minute. Would you mind explaining what you were doing going 80 miles an hour? At night. On a

Baja highway?" In the first place, the damned van wouldn't go 80 miles an hour.

"That's the speed limit. Eighty. Didn't you notice the signs when you were driving down?"

I sighed and stood up and banged my head on the roof.

Anya held the flashlight while I wrestled with the tire iron. I struggled to loosen the nuts and ended up with a scraped knuckle and a good bit of cursing under my breath for my efforts. Once the nuts were loose, I finished jacking up the front end. The tire came off fast and I replaced it with the spare. I lowered the jack and cursed out loud again.

"It's low on air. We need to find a llantera."

"What's that?" she wanted to know.

"Llantera. Two Ls. It's a tire shop. They're usually right beside the road. It'll have a sign with white lettering painted on. Keep your eyes open."

I rolled the flat around the back and loaded the jack and the tire before completing a walk-around. It wasn't so bad. The right headlight was out and there was a bit of a dent, but it was no big deal. We could get back on the road, at least.

"You should have pulled over and woke me up, Anya. It's not safe driving on these roads at night."

"Fine. You can drive from now on."

Here we go again, just when I thought I'd broken her of that habit. I bit my tongue. It wasn't her fault. I was the negligent adult in the room.

"The 80 on the signs means eighty kilometers an hour. Mexico is metric. So is Canada if you're ever up that way.

She looked across at me in the dim light from the dashboard. "So that's like, umm—"

"Fifty miles an hour."

"Fifty? Seriously? We'll never get to the border at that rate."

Maybe not, but there was no way I was going 80 miles an hour on a narrow Mexican highway in the black of night. "Yeah, no. I'll drive from now on, okay? It's your turn to sleep."

Anya crawled into the back without complaint and I figured she'd fall off just as hard as I had. I stopped thinking about it when the hand-painted sign reflected in the van's solitary headlight. I pulled into the dusty parking lot and parked. I banged on the door to the llantera and a nervous older man came out, looking sleepy and disheveled.

"I'm sorry I got you out of bed. I need some air, señor."

He mumbled and nodded and uncoiled an air hose and I was back in business.

"Would you like a headlight for the one that is burned out?" he asked.

Why not? He could use the business, and I could use the headlight. "Si. Gracias."

That took another few minutes to install and I left him with a healthy tip to brighten his night for disturbing his sleep. The light pointed down in front of the van, but at least I wouldn't get pulled over for having only one headlight. And then I wondered if that ever happened in Mexico.

FIFTY-EIGHT

I had to stop. I had no choice. I needed gas. I woke Anya and asked her to fill the tank while I went in to pay. On the way I picked up a couple of burritos and some drinks.

That's when it hit the fan. In broad daylight. But this was Mexico. I wouldn't have expected anything less. There were two of them. I sprinted to the van under a hail of gunfire. Anya held the sliding door open. She wrestled the AK out from beneath the foamy and was holding it. A banana hung from the underside. She handed it off.

"Good job. You're hired. Now hop over the tin and hit go."

"Where am I going? Where am I going?" Panic rose in her voice.

"Tecate. Turn right and follow the signs. It'll be another right onto a paved highway. Now breathe."

I could hear Anya panting as I kicked open the rear door and then nothing as the sound of air and open road assaulted my ears. I yelled at her. "Don't stop for anything. Keep going."

"Where? Going where?"

I yelled back at her. "La frontera. Look for the green

highway signs. They're just like back home."

We swung onto the highway. The van wallowed. I hung on for life. The rocking and rolling ended as we settled onto the pavement. I kicked the door open again. I expected to see an army of vehicles in hot pursuit.

A single black SUV came up fast. Anya made the final turn onto the highway to the border. The van rocked from side to side.

"You're doing a great job. Watch for a red building on the left. It'll say bombero. Go past it."

"Bombero? What the hell is a bombero?"

"Fire department. Keep going past it to la frontera. Follow the signs. Keep your head down. You're sitting in front of armor plate."

Lead slammed against steel. The sound reverberated in the closed van. César had done a good job.

"See what I mean? You're safe up there." I looked to make sure. The steering wheel turned magically, guided by invisible hands. "Good girl. Keep down."

I thought I heard an arf. The van bumped and rocked as Anya steered as best she could from her crouched position. I let go of the open door. I steadied and aimed and repositioned as Anya swerved past a car. The SUV chasing us didn't break its stride. I dropped to a knee, aimed, and fired a burst at the radiator. A single orange tracer told me I hit my mark.

The door slammed shut, blocking my fire. I twisted the handle and kicked it open, holding it with a foot. I aimed another burst at the windshield. The SUV swerved and crossed a parking lot. It crashed into a building and halted. No one got out.

"Shit. I'm hit."

"What?"

"I'm hit. I'm hit."

She slowed and a second SUV gained ground. I fired another short burst, followed by a longer one. The SUV turned and careened onto a side street.

"They're done. Pull over. We have to ditch the AK."

I tossed it out the door and pulled it closed. I rustled up a shirt and buttoned it over my wound. Blood seeped through.

"You're hurt. Jimmy. You're bleeding."

"Not now. Keep your eyes on the road. Pull over and let me drive. You sit in the passenger seat and smile at the nice border guard. That's your job now. Sit and be nice and friendly and remember I'm your step-dad, just like we rehearsed on the way down. Okay?"

She was shaking again. I couldn't blame her. "Breathe. In. Out. In. Out. Passports. Get our passports."

I pulled over a second time. Should I toss the handgun too? I didn't have time. I was getting woozy. Come on, girl. Get the passports. Get the passports.

"Found them." She slammed the door and got in the front and we were off.

"Remember."

"I know. I know. I'm scared," she said.

"We'll be home in no time. You can count on it."

She looked from me to the blood beginning to seep through the fresh shirt. "That doesn't look so good, Jimmy."

"Yeah, just so you know. I'm scared too. Here we go."

I halted at the line. It took forever while we waited. Anya's breathing came in short gasps.

"Breathe. In. Out. In, out, mija."

"Mija?"

"Yes. Daughter. Mija."

The wave to approach came. I pulled up and halted beside the border guard's station. I struggled to work the lever into Park. Anya leaned over and looked across at him and smiled. I fumbled with the passports and passed them out the window.

"It's great to be home but I think I picked up some kind of a stomach bug."

The agent laughed before bending to look into the van. "Yeah, I hear that a lot. You don't look so good if you don't mind me saying."

He looked to the girl in the seat beside me. "Is that your daughter? Anya Quinn, is it?

She looked at the man and smiled.

"My step-daughter. Yes. And you got her name right."

Out of the corner of my eye I caught Anya beaming an even bigger smile in the guard's direction.

"All right." The officer handed our passports back. "You're free to go. There's a store up the road a bit if you need anything."

"Thanks. I'll be stopping." I put the van in gear. The transmission caught suddenly and jerked and I struggled to control the van.

"Wait. Stop!"

Anya craned her neck to look back at the guard. She

made a grab for the seatback and almost slipped onto the floor. "Oh shit. Jimmy—"

"Be cool. Let's see what he wants. Just be cool." I backed up to the booth and fought with the gear lever to get the van into Park again. "What is it?" I asked.

"Your license plate. It's almost falling off."

"Thanks, Officer. I'll be sure to take a look at it when I stop."

FIFTY-NINE

The border guard turned his attention to the next vehicle. Sweat poured down my back. Anya trembled uncontrollably.

"That was close. There should be a store just ahead. We need—"

"I know what we need. Sit tight. And get in the back, Jim. If you pass out I won't be able to get you there."

I made it into the back on my own while Anya went into the store. I retrieved the handgun from its hiding place and slipped a magazine into it. I groaned and collapsed on the foamy as Anya slid the door open and tossed in bags filled with—filled with— what the hell, I didn't care.

She cut my shirt off and poured alcohol over my wound. "If you didn't have those love handles—"

"Excuse me, but please don't refer to my muffin top as love handles."

"Uh-huh."

She doused me in alcohol. I groaned my discontent. "Shut up and take it. I'm the boss of you now, mister detective. You got me home. Now it's my job to get you home. We need a hospital."

"No hospital. We can't. It's a gunshot wound. They have to report it. I'll end up chained to a bed and you'll get turned over to child welfare. Did I say no hospital?"

"I will not. I'm over 18 now. How soon you forget."

"No hospital. What did you get to cover up the wound?"

She turned the grocery store bags upside down. Pads and tampons tumbled onto the floor.

"Those tampons aren't any good. You can't put—"

She looked at me and scowled.

"Oh. Sorry. I was thinking—"

"Don't think. Shut up and watch me work." Anya poured alcohol on a pad and taped it to the front of the wound. She lifted with her hand and I rolled to let her see my back. She taped it, too.

"The bullet went in the front and came out the back. It must have been the one that made the noise," she said.

"It's called a through-and-through. In and out. Kinda like breathing, only quicker. Clean, too. No lead to pick out."

"I'm going back to get more gauze. And pads. And alcohol."

"See if they've got something to drink, too."

"Water?" she asked.

"No. Booze. Nice and strong."

Anya returned and tossed the bags over the seat into the back. The bottle clattered to the floor. "She checked my ID. I used my Florida driver's license."

"Good for you. Shit, woman. Don't smash good liquor. It is good, right?"

"Tequila. Take it and sing me a song or I'll throw it out."

The van jerked into gear and we were off. At least it wasn't a standard shift.

"Oh. I almost forgot."

"Now what, Jimmy?"

"There's a handgun tucked into the passenger seat. All you have to do is rack and aim."

"Thanks. I think."

"Teamwork makes it dreamwork."

I pictured her eyes rolling and smiled. I chased after the tequila bottle on the floor and cracked the seal. It was good. I broke into song.

"Ninety-nine bottles of beer..."

SIXTY

Anya struggled with the razor she fished out of her backpack and began her first attempt at shaving Jim. The razor scraped and caught on stubble and scraped again. She dipped it in alcohol and went back to work.

"You are a stubborn man, Jimmy Nash. Maddie isn't going to care what you look like, you know. I think she's going to be happy you're home."

"You don't know her. I want to look good in my coffin when she kills me."

"Yeah, yeah. She'll give you a hug and a smooch on the cheek and take you to the hospital. Like I should have." Her voice went up several octaves and she almost screamed the last. "There. All done."

She sat back and admired her handiwork and was glad she didn't have a mirror to show her work. She doused a paper towel with alcohol and dabbed at his face. The bleeding was almost stopped.

"Okay. We gotta hit the road. We're almost there, Jimmy."

He didn't answer. He was out again. She checked his forehead. It was sweaty and hot. Fever. He had a fever.

She considered a hospital. They'd passed one. All she would have to do is turn around.

But she knew where she was, too. She'd been on trips with her mom and dad into the city. It was a piece of cake to find Jimmy's office. She could almost see it. Well, she knew the street, at least. All she had to do was find it and drive south.

Anya burned a U-turn across traffic. Horns honked. Brakes squealed. She reversed and straightened the wheel and gunned the gas pedal into the parking spot. The heavy van's brakes chose that instant to give out and she crashed into an old car parked in front of the building.

"We're home, Jimmy."

Jim didn't answer. She pushed at the heavy door and got out and ran around the front of the van. An old, huge-ass ugly car blocked her way. She backtracked around the back to the side door. She yanked the handle and the door squeaked and rattled against the stops with a bang.

"Come on, Jimmy." She slapped at his swollen face. "Shit. I knew I shouldn't have shaved you with the razor I use for my legs."

His eyes opened and rolled. "What was that?"

"Nothing, Jimmy. We're home."

"The bags. Get the bags," he insisted. She could barely hear him.

"Never mind the fucking bags," she almost screamed.

The building's door crashed open and a big black dog bounded out. He was followed by two women.

"Maddie?"

The dog beat the women to the van and came to a sliding halt. He sniffed and snorted and a woman wearing some kind of costume ran up to the van. The other one bent to Jimmy. The dog bared his teeth. The woman called to him to heel and sit and he moved to sit on the curb. His tail didn't wag. He wouldn't stop looking at her and growling.

"I brought Jimmy home," she announced.

SIXTY-ONE

I convinced Maddie to go on a secret mission to pick up something special for Anya. I explained what it was about, and she laughed and thought it was a great idea. "I never knew that. In that case, I think I'll get us some extras." She came back and placed them in our room's closet beside the others. "I wonder which ones she'll choose."

I didn't have long to wait. Anya returned with her mother in tow. She made introductions and the pair settled on Anya's bed. "I've been released, Jimmy. I'm going home."

"That's great to hear, mija. You take care now. Stay safe."

"No problemo, Jimmy. It's all good."

I rubbed at my face while her mother thanked me for getting her daughter home safe. I was the one who was most grateful, even if my face was still a mess thanks to Anya's skill with a dull razor.

"Don't worry, Jimmy. Your face will be like new in no time." Anya turned to her mother. "He made me shave him before I got him home to Maddie. He told me he wanted to look good when she put him in the coffin."

"Oh Anya. Jim wouldn't say anything like that. You're exaggerating."

"Maybe." She grinned at me.

Anya made for the closet to collect her things. She opened the door and slammed it shut, and opened it again, slowly, as though not believing her eyes. She kicked off the fancy whites and donned the black.

"So long, Jimmy."

"Not so fast, woman. It takes me a bit to get my feet on the floor." I groaned and she rushed to help me sit up. "What am I going to do now? There's no one to prop me up."

Maddie and Friday chose that moment to enter the hospital room. Friday scampered to Jim's bed and sniffed and snuffled at the girl's fingers. Satisfied, he plopped himself down on the floor by the bed and woofed to let everyone know he was the one on duty now.

"It looks to me like you've got all the help you need." The girl collected her backpack and danced toward the door in her black Air Force 1s.

I tried not to grin. "Girl, you are bad-ass!"

Anya's mother blushed and followed behind her daughter. She checked the closet where she noticed a pair "of white sneakers. "Now Jim. Don't encourage her. Dear, what about your other shoes?

Anya hesitated at the door. "They're not mine, Mom. They belong to someone else." She turned to look over her shoulder. "We'll always have Cabo, Jimmy."

I forced myself up and limped to the window. Anya and her mother were on their way to the car. They had their arms around each other, and Anya was gesticulating with her free hand. She halted and removed her backpack to unzip it before going through it. She halted and zipped it up.

She looked up at the window. Spotted me. Grinned a toothy grin and waved frantically.

It was about time she found it.

SIXTY-TWO

Maddie made her way to the kitchen. A door slammed down the hall and Emma came through the apartment door. Friday sat patiently, waiting for his breakfast bowl.

"Come and get it or I'll throw it out."

"Are you making your famous grilled cheese sammiches, Jim? The ones with the tomato and bacon?" Emma wanted to know.

"That I am."

I passed Emma her plate. She took it and waited patiently for Maddie to get hers. Friday looked up at me, hopeful as ever. I set his bowl down and he woofed his appreciation. He was the first to voice his displeasure with a whine and a soulful look in my direction.

"Sorry, dog, but Maddie says we're on a strict diet. No chopped bacon for you."

Emma bit into her sandwich and her face lit up as she groaned her pleasure. "James, this is a delish delight to my country palate."

"You're welcome, Emma. Any time."

Maddie took a bite and hesitated before she began chewing. I knelt to pet Friday while I kept watch out of the corner of my eye. Maddie frowned and set her sandwich on the plate. "I didn't get any bacon in mine, Jim. Did you forget?"

Friday snorted and backed away from me. He was disappointed, too.

"You said you were putting us on a strict diet. That means no more treats like crunchy bacon crumblings in our grilled cheese sandwiches. And no more bacon for Friday."

The dog heard his name and looked at his mistress.

"Oh come on. I meant no more for you and Friday, not no more for me. Emma has bacon in hers."

Friday recognized the word bacon and put two and two together before snorting his displeasure. Emma knew when to run. "I have some paperwork to get caught up on. I'll see you all later."

She made a grab for her plate and rushed out of the apartment. Friday remembered how easy it was to get treats from Emma and moved to scurry after her.

His mistress called after him. "Friday. Get back here. You're not scamming Emma out of her bacon."

The dog hung his head and moved to sit beside me. We were in the same doghouse now. I backed up to the stove and grabbed the frying pan. I slid the bacon grilled cheese I had waiting onto Maddie's plate. I slipped the rest of the bacon into Friday's bowl. Satisfied, he woofed his thanks and began devouring his breakfast.

"Anything you say, dear. Right, Friday?"

Friday wasn't paying attention. He was busy enjoying his treat.

JIM NASH READ ORDER

Marina Mystery

Twisted Sisters

Sleeping with a .45

Pirate Cay

Thrill Kill Jill

Greetings From Key West

Lost Paradise

No Angels

Mexico Gamble

No Picnic

Fallen Angels

Vendetta

A Girl's Best Friend

Dead End

No Harbor

Dog Days

Startup Blues

Last Stop to Nowhere

The Last Goodbye

Revenge Is Justice

Escape

Wedding Bell Blues

Breakdown

Little Girl Lost

Forget Me Not

All The Glitter

Mexico Time

Partners In Crime

Shop Till You Drop

Lobo

No Free Ride

Gone

Seasonal

Trick or Treat

Helping Santa

Jim Nash Investigates

The Snap Brim Fedora Caper

The Lady in White

PRINT BOOKS

Jim Nash The Beginning
Gun Crazy
Gun Crazy 2
Gun Crazy 3
Fallen Angels
Last Stop to Nowhere
Revenge is Justice
Escape / Forget Me Not
Wedding Bell Blues / Breakdown
Forget Me Not
Mexico Time
LOBO
No Free Ride / Gone
Stealing America
No Escape
Blame It on Djibouti
Trouble in Paradise
Nash & Delaney Collide

Dead Reckoning
Lie Cheat Steal
Uncharted
Go-Around
Sand Storm
Harry Delaney Collection

No Way Out
Bad Girls
Bank Robber Dames

The Last President

About the Author

Peter Duke is a Canadian author. He resides and writes in a small college town in the Province of Ontario.

Aviator. Motorcycle rider. Vagabond. Drifter. Trouble-maker. Jack of all trades and master of none. I've been riding and writing about the places I've been and the people I've seen for a few years now. Some of my writing is factual; some of it isn't. I like to leave it up to readers to decide which lies are the truth.

pxduke.com | peterxduke@gmail.com

Check out all six books of the Harry Delaney Adventure series. Find out why Harry makes his way from the North African desert to the Mexican Baja. Discover how he ends up having a triumphal return to the deserts of North Africa.